The Boca Babe did a head-to-toe body scan, eyeing me disdainfully.

I think there's a factory somewhere in Boca Raton that stamps these Babes out in bulk—long blond hair, fake boobs and all. Boca Babes Unlimited. Sometimes I can't believe I used to be one of them myself.

What had I been thinking? Oh, yeah, that money can buy happiness.

Okay, maybe I'm a little tough on the Babes now, or maybe it's really myself I'm tough on. I mean, if that was your past, would you want to face it every day—or would you run from it, like the Plague, as I do?

Miriam Auerbach

Miriam Auerbach was born in Prague, Czechoslovakia. The first of many changes in her life occurred at age six, when she witnessed tanks rolling past her family's home during the Soviet occupation of 1968. Shortly thereafter, her family fled to the United States, taking her with them. She grew up in Denver, where she spent her high school and early college years studying diligently to become a particle physicist. However, during a brief stint at Los Alamos National Lab, she began to suspect that building nuclear weapons just might not be the best way to spend her life. Thus, at age twenty she rebelled and spent the next decade living on the fringes of the Harley biker world (in the days before it was overtaken by middle-aged professionals).

In her thirties she returned to semiconventional life, earning a Ph.D. in social work and becoming a university professor. In this capacity, under the name of Miriam Potocky-Tripodi, she has taught legions of students and written a slew of academic treatises crusading for social justice for the world's dispossessed. She has found this to be a rewarding career, with the minor exception that one fine day she crashed headfirst into the glass ceiling of the ivory tower. Falling into a funk, she took to her bed to eat chocolates and watch old Dirty Harry movies. She didn't get Harry's appeal until she suddenly had a vision of him as a woman, and then it all made sense. Thus her debut novel, *Dirty Harriet*, was born.

Miriam lives in Boca Raton, Florida, with her husband and killer Corgi, Elvira. She continues to profess by day and decompress by night by writing her next Dirty Harriet mystery. Visit her at www.miriamauerbach.com.

DIRTY HARRIET

MIRIAM
AUERBACH

In Loving Memory
Pavel Potocky/Ruben Auerbach
1924–2003

"Our revels now are ended. These our actors,
As I foretold you, were all spirits and
Are melted into air, into thin air:
And, like the baseless fabric of this vision,
The cloud-capp'd towers, the gorgeous palaces,
The solemn temples, the great globe itself,
Yea, all which it inherit, shall dissolve
And, like this insubstantial pageant faded,
Leave not a rack behind. We are such stuff
As dreams are made on, and our little life
Is rounded with a sleep."
—William Shakespeare, *The Tempest* IV, i

Big-time thanks to: Paige Wheeler and Lisa VanAuken of Creative Media Agency; Darcy Lunsford and group members of the creative writing workshop at Spanish River Community High School Adult Education Program, 2003; Carol Cail of 2nd Draft Professional Writing Reviews; Barbara Parker and group members (Deanne Miller, Michael Stephan, Vance Bradley, Andrew Kingston) of the 3rd Degree Thursday at Sleuthfest, 2004; and Tara Gavin, Julie Barrett and everyone at Harlequin.

To Tom Gregoire,
for setting me straight on all things Harley.

To my female posse, Karen Dodge, Gail Ukockis, Nan Van Den Bergh and Andrea LeBoss—you chicks rock! And to my husband, Tony Tripodi, for your steadfast support.

I confess. I said it. When my husband raised his fists at me that last time, I said, "Go ahead, make my day!"

He obliged. So did I, putting a .44 Magnum bullet through his heart and putting him out of my misery. Permanently.

Hey, it was a clear case of self-defense, as attested to by the five hundred witnesses at the scene, a wedding reception at the Boca Raton Beach Club (BaR-B-Cue for short). Okay, so I ruined the bride's big day. Give me a break, will you? The SOB had it coming, trust me.

Well, the press had a field day, dubbing me "Dirty Harriet" in honor of Clint Eastwood's notorious Dirty Harry character. That suits me fine—there are a lot of similarities between old Harry and me. We both speak softly and carry a big gun.

My real name is Harriet Horowitz. I'm a recovering Boca Babe. No, those aren't the opening lines of a Boca Babes Anonymous meeting. There is no such beast, and even if there were, groups aren't my bag.

So what's to recover from, you ask? Let's start with personal appearance. The Boca Babe needs: a weekly manicure, biweekly pedicure, monthly highlighting and razor-edge trimming, lip and brow waxing, bikini waxing, a truckload of cosmetics to keep Estée Lauder and Lancôme in business, twice-weekly trips to the mall with the personal shopper, daily sessions with the personal trainer. Had enough? We haven't even started on household maintenance.

The Boca Babe must be in possession of a McMansion—the six-bedroom, five-bath faux Mediterranean palazzo situated in one of the euphemistically named "gated communities" (translation: walled fortresses). And does this household take care of itself? Of course not. You need a gardener, a housekeeper, a pool service person—minimum. Those are your regulars. Then there's the other help you call in for special occasions, such as hosting your son's bar mitzvah or your parents' golden anniversary. This requires a party planner, a caterer, a wardrobe consultant. Well, you get the picture.

Now, let's face it, most women cannot acquire all of this themselves. But there's one surefire way to achieve this fairy tale, and that's to marry a rich American prince.

My prince was named Bruce. I'd met him when I was attending one of those prissy women's colleges up in New England. My mom had sent me there, not to get any useful education, mind you, just to become the right kind of woman to snare the right kind of man. And Bruce was it. He was a law student at Yale. He was hot, smart, charming, connected and soon to be rich. A budding Boca Babe's dream. Sure, there were the usual warning signs of incipient abuse—the moodiness, the possessiveness, the volatility. But just like most women, I didn't put two and two together, or maybe I repressed whatever doubts I may have had, because I just had to have him. After all, you can't be a Boca Babe if you're man-less.

I brought Bruce home to Mom in Boca. She thoroughly approved, so we got married and started living the high life. Bruce became an associate, then a partner, in Boca's leading law firm, representing pharmaceutical companies, health insurance companies and the tobacco industry against people who claimed they'd suffered injury or loss of a loved one due to the corporations' negligence or malfeasance. Was it lucrative? Hell, yes. Moral? I didn't want to go there. I was too busy spending the money. Every time a little voice of conscience started nagging at me, I'd suppress it by going on a shopping spree with my friends.

While I was shopping, Bruce was working and hanging with Boca's power brokers, fueling his energy and ego with cocaine. And as his blow use increased, so did his blowups and put-downs. In his eyes I'd gone from being a brainy babe to a babbling bimbo. Pretty soon the shoving, slapping, hitting and kicking started. But while he was addicted to the coke, I was addicted to the money and the image it brought. So for ten years I put up with his verbal and physical abuse to "Keep Up Appearances."

My road to liberation started when my personal trainer suggested I take up the Israeli martial art Krav Maga to get my ass into shape. In the process of toning my backside, something else happened. I began to grow a backbone. As my self-defense skills increased, I started to ask myself: Did I really need to be a punching bag in order to keep the McMansion, the Mercedes, the manicures, the whole shebang? For that matter, did I really need the McMansion, the Mercedes, the manicures and the whole shebang in the first place?

Yeah, I know what you're thinking: why didn't I just divorce the schmuck—did I have to whack him? Easier said than done. You know the story. I left a couple times, he came and dragged me back, threatening to kill not only me but my mom if I ever left again. And then there was the response of the cops and the courts.

One time Bruce was arrested after he threw me to the ground outside a five-star restaurant. But he was buddies with the police chief, who personally went to the jail at three a.m. to release him and drop the charges. Another time he beat me so badly I had to go to the hospital. We almost made it to court on that charge, but then the hospital records documenting my injuries mysteriously disappeared, and the case was dismissed for lack of evidence.

By then Bruce had incurred some serious debts with his drug habit. Some really shady characters started hounding him. Bruce bought himself a gun. He just didn't figure that someday I'd use it on him. Neither did I. Until that night.

That was four years ago, when I was thirty-five. After the shooting, I spent a few nights in the county jail overlooking Donald Trump's golf course in West Palm. Finally, the D.A. decided it was justifiable homicide and let me go. So, I unloaded my Boca Babe lifestyle—the house, the car, the clothes, everything—and decided to start over as far from there as I could. Well, inasmuch as I hate winter and love Florida, I didn't venture all that far. Just to the edge of the Everglades.

Now, home is a two-room wood cabin up on stilts in the Glades just west of Boca. Basically, I've moved from swank to swamp. You know that magazine you see in checkout lines at the grocery store, *Real Simple?* That's just for starters. I'm talking the real thing. No electricity lines (just my generator), no land phone (just my cell) and no neighbors (just Lana, the six-foot gator that lurks around my front porch). No roads, either—just my airboat.

Now, if all that seems like a drastic change, it is. Here's why: with any kind of recovery, you've got to go cold turkey. You've got to change playgrounds and playmates. There's no doing it half-assed, or you get sucked right back in to where you started. So I had to reinvent my life. And just moving to a different city wouldn't cut it. I wanted to meet the challenge of total independence.

The only obstacle was money. I had no kids—neither of us had ever wanted them—so that's one worry I didn't have. But as a Boca Babe, I'd spent my husband's income as fast as it came in. And he did, too. Even the house was mortgaged to the hilt. So I was left with nothing but my jewelry, which I sold to buy my one treat to myself, my Hog—a 2003 100th anniversary 883cc Harley Hugger. That Evolution engine represents my own personal evolution. For some people there's therapy, for me there's my Hog.

Anyway, I needed to support myself, so I went back to school and learned some skills for real life, as opposed to the twisted fairy tale I'd been living. Then I answered an ad in the paper for someone with computer skills, which turned out to be for a private eye agency, doing skip traces and background checks. When my boss learned that I also possessed a whole slew of Boca Babe skills, he sent me out on cases as a decoy, enticing cheating husbands into making a pass, then getting the whole thing on tape. It was pretty sleazy, but it gave me start in the business. A year or so later I was able to get my own license and open my own agency, ScamBusters. And I set out to expose the steamy underbelly of Boca.

I've been in business a little over a year now, and let me tell you, it's booming. Boca has scams aplenty. This is South Florida, after all. You didn't think all that crisp new money floating around here was earned by honest hard work, did you? Insurance scams, investment scams, immigration scams—you name it, we've got it.

But the last thing I expected that February day when the Contessa von Phul walked into my office was a murder case. I guess even I hadn't known just how ugly things could get in beautiful Boca Raton.

CHAPTER 1

The contessa walked into my office on a Tuesday clad in Chanel from head to toe—the pink suit with white trim, the pearls, the black-toed shoes, the white quilted bag with the chain strap—with her Chihuahua, Coco, ensconced on her left arm. The scent of Chanel No. 19 wafted in with her. Eau de parfum, eau de dog and eau de dollars hit me at once. My sinuses rebelled immediately and I went into a sneezing fit.

Glancing around imperiously at my barren office as she flipped back her mahogany pageboy hair, the contessa pronounced, "Harriet, what you need in here is some foliage. You know, the leaves will absorb the toxins, oxygenate the air, clear those allergies right up."

I just love it when people tell me what I need, don't you? She could take that little rodent-disguised-as-a-canine and—

"Yes, Your Excellency," I said. I learned long ago that you don't mess with the contessa. She was aris-

tocracy, after all. The Boca version, that is. Her true
origins were unknown. Whether she had acquired her
title through birth, marriage, or purchase, no one
knew. There was no count in her present, and she
didn't speak of her past. Many believed that she had
to be the real thing, since who would actually pay for
a name like von Phul? Personally, I wasn't so sure. I
happened to know she was a crafty one—she could
well have bought the name, figuring people would
think exactly that—there was no way anyone would
buy it. Faking everyone out with a double negative,
so to speak.

I knew the contessa from my former Boca Babe life.
We had served on several charity committees together.
She was the senior version of the Boca Babe—the
Botox Babe. Seventy going on fifty. Yep, we have some
of the world's best surgeons right here in Boca.

She hadn't finished with her critique of my lifestyle
yet. Her eyes did a full-body scan as she checked me
out. A Babe compulsion—they just can't help themselves. She took in my buff butt and biceps, big boobs,
big dark hair and big dark eyes. She did miss my big-
ass Smith & Wesson Magnum .44 gun, which I had
license to carry concealed and kept stashed in
my boot.

"It wouldn't hurt you to spiff up your wardrobe a little," she declared, peering at me down her hawkish nose.

I had on my usual post-Babe uniform—all black, all stretch tank top and boot-cut leggings. She clearly wasn't impressed.

"I've simplified, Contessa," I replied. "Besides, S and L are a girl's best friends."

She looked confused. Her brow would have wrinkled, but the Botox wouldn't let it.

"Savings and Loans?" she asked.

"No—Spandex and Lycra."

She rolled her green eyes and looked around for a place to sit.

She brushed some imaginary dog hairs off of one of the two Naugahyde chairs in front of my desk and gingerly placed Coco on it. Coco did a body shake and deposited some non-imaginary hairs. The contessa settled her tall frame into the other seat.

"Harriet, I have a case for you," she said, cutting to the chase. "An unsolved murder."

"But Contessa," I said, "I don't do murder. I do scams. My motto is 'They scam 'em, I slam 'em.'"

"But Harriet," she said, "this is a case that cries out for justice. And you are just the person for it."

"Why is that?" I asked, astounded.

"You will care about this case like no one else. You won't let go until you've solved it, because a part of the victim is a part of you."

"Oh, yeah? Which part is that?"

"That's for you to discover."

She was trying to get to me, I could tell. And she was succeeding, damn her.

"Go ahead," I said grudgingly.

"As you well know, I am benefactress of the Central American Rescue Mission."

How could I not know? For that matter, how could anyone in Boca not know? The contessa's name and face were plastered all over the place promoting her pet charity. She was in the papers, in *Boca Raton* magazine, on flyers in the Publix grocery, everywhere. The Central American Rescue Mission provided assistance to refugees who had fled to Florida from the war-torn countries of the south. The contessa's interest was thought to derive from her own childhood experiences in wartime Europe, though of course no one really knew.

"Maybe you remember from the papers, Harriet, that one of my girls was killed about a year ago," she continued. All the Rescue Mission's clients were her "girls" and "boys."

"Yes, I do vaguely remember something. A body was found in the tomato fields west of here?"

"Not a *body*," she admonished. "A *person*. Gladys Gutierrez. Yes, they found the poor soul strangled last February. Just think of the irony, Harriet. This sweet girl had escaped the killing fields of Guatemala only to wind up dead in the tomato fields of South Florida. And she was just on the verge of starting a new life. She was learning English, she'd just gotten a new job, her future was bright. Tell me, where is the justice in that?"

"What about the police?" I asked.

"Well, of course they tried. But you know how it is. More pressing matters came up, and Gladys has been shelved."

I knew what she was talking about. Boca had been rocked by a few upper-crust scandals lately. The former president of the local public university had been accused of accepting a brand new red Corvette bought with university foundation money that had been laundered through his wife's interior decorator, while the local private college was accused of illegally procuring cadavers for its funeral services program without the families' consent. So I could see how a pesky little problem like the murder of a Guatemalan refugee had taken a back seat.

"I didn't want to interfere with the official investigation," the contessa continued, "but it's been a year now, and I had my own internal deadline. I decided I'd give the police that long, and if they didn't make an arrest by now, I'd take matters into my own hands. Now I'm putting it in yours."

There were plenty of other P.I.s in town she could have picked. But she was getting to me. I could see the writing on the wall—if I didn't solve this case, no one ever would. Not that I have an ego or anything.

There was another thing, too. I figured I kind of owed the contessa. When I'd been in the slammer after offing my husband, most of my Boca Babe friends had dumped me like toxic waste, but not the contessa. She had been one of the few to visit me, and had even made public statements in my defense. In fact, I sometimes wondered if she'd had anything to do with the charges being dropped.

"Okay, I'll consider the case," I muttered.

"Of course you will," she said. She whipped a sheaf of papers out of her Chanel bag. "Here is a copy of the police summary of the case. I will see you at the Rescue Mission tomorrow morning at nine." She picked up Coco and headed for the door.

The gall! She had obviously decided before even

coming in that I would take the case. I glared out the iron bars covering the plate-glass window as she pulled out in her Rolls.

I took a deep breath. The contessa had put her faith in me, big-time. No one had ever done that before. Trust me to attract someone's adulterous husband? Sure. Catch a con artist? Sure. But solve a murder? Not. The contessa was putting me to the test, and I had to meet the challenge. I couldn't let her down.

It was getting late in the day so I decided to pack it in and head home. I would read the case file tonight. I shut down my computer, turned out the lights and stepped outside. I locked the door, then the wrought-iron gate that serves as my security.

My office is located on the seedy side of Boca. Yeah, there is one. Of course you knew that everything glitzy in life is just a facade. Boca's backside, or at least one of them, is along its southwestern edge, on Highway 441, technically outside the city limits. This is strip mall city, with rutted parking lots and dusty barren roadways in place of the manicured hedges and fairways to the east. ScamBusters is in one of these strips, wedged between Tony's Tattoos and Carl's Checks 'R' Us check-cashing store.

Actually, the location is a business advantage. Think about it. My typical clients from east Boca wouldn't be caught dead walking into ScamBusters, since that would be tantamount to a public announcement that they'd been conned. So by driving a couple miles out of town, they don't have to worry about being seen and having their country club know their business the next day. Here, all they have to worry about is getting their Mercedes or their Beemers carjacked.

I put on my leather jacket, chaps, gloves and helmet, and settled into the seat of my Hog. I turned the ignition key and pushed the starter button, and the engine roared to life. I pushed my way back out of the parking space, then opened up the throttle and took off. As I headed west on Glades Road and left the traffic behind, everything faded out of my consciousness except the familiar four-stroke rhythm of the V-twin engine. You know that sound—the one you get only from a Harley. But maybe you don't know the feel. Let me put it this way: it's a five-hundred-pound vibrator between your legs. And people wonder why a woman would ride a bike.

My airboat was docked at the road's end. At that point, civilization stopped and the wilderness took over. It was the place where solid ground gave way to uncertainty. The swamp—neither earth nor water—that murky no-man's-land that was my home.

I pulled down the loading ramp and rolled the Hog onto the boat. It's one of those big mothers originally used for toting tourists that's been specially adapted to carry my bike. I sat in the boat's driver's seat. I pushed my foam earplugs into my ears, then donned my soundproofing earmuffs over those. This sucker is loud. I started the engine and the huge rear-mounted fan began its frenzied spin. I shifted into gear and the boat took off, the sawgrass seemingly parting before me as I moved ahead.

Two miles due northwest, I reached my cabin. I pulled the boat up to the porch, disembarked and tied the craft to the hitching post. My own Wild West. I walked into the combination living room/dining room/kitchen and pulled my boots off. At the kitchen cabinet, I took out my lead crystal glass—one of the few remnants of my past life, so I guess I'm not fully recovered yet—and poured myself a shot of Hennessy. I went out to the porch to sit in my rocking chair and watch the sun set. I spotted Lana, the gator, lurking a few yards off to my left.

"Hi, honey, I'm home," I called. "How was your day?"

She didn't respond.

I pulled out the case summary the contessa had given me to "think over."

There wasn't a whole lot there. The body of a female thought to be in her early twenties had been found in a tomato field outside of Boca on February 19. Exactly one year ago. The victim had been killed by strangulation. Bruise marks around her throat indicated something had been wrapped around it and tightened. She had been dead about four days when her body was discovered.

The crime scene investigation turned up no murder weapon at the scene. Because of heavy rain in the intervening days between the death and the discovery of the body, the crime scene did not provide any further reliable forensic evidence. It was not known whether the death had occurred at the scene or whether the victim had been killed elsewhere and then dumped in the tomato field.

The summary included several crime scene photos. The victim's body lay facedown in the mud, twisted and crumpled. Her clothes were a simple brown skirt and tan sweater, both soaked through and mud-streaked. But it was her shoes that really got to me. They, too, were mud-covered, but bright white patches of canvas shone through. They looked brand-new. The idea that this woman had just bought a shining new pair of sneakers, probably in hopes of a brighter future, only to wear them once or twice before being brutally murdered, sent a stab of pain right through my gut.

There were also some autopsy photos. In these, the victim lay on a cold steel slab. Her pale face seemed remarkably untouched and peaceful, in contrast with the trauma marks around her neck. Again, I felt a wave of sickness at the clearly vicious attack on such a young, innocent-looking woman.

I resumed reading. The tomato fields were home to many Guatemalan immigrants who worked on the local farms. The police had taken one of the autopsy photos of the victim around to the homes where the immigrants lived. The victim was identified as Gladys Gutierrez by a friend, Eulalia Lopez. Working with a Spanish interpreter, the police questioned Eulalia but she was unable to provide any solid leads on the murder.

The police interviewed the farm workers' crew boss, Jake Lamont, who stated that Gladys had worked in the fields and lived in the company housing until about two weeks previously. Then she had disappeared and he didn't know where she had gone. The police talked with a few of the other residents, but they said they didn't know much about Gladys.

According to the summary, after the story of Gladys's murder appeared in the local paper with a request that anyone with information contact the police, the contessa had called them. She informed them that Gladys had been a client at the Central American Rescue Mission and that the mission had placed Gladys in a live-in housekeeping job, which is why she had left the tomato fields. The contessa provided the police with what little she knew about Gladys, but she had no information that could help solve the case.

The police then interviewed Gladys's new employer, Tricia Weinstein. She stated that Gladys had disappeared from the home on February 15. Tricia had not reported Gladys as a missing person because she assumed that Gladys had simply bailed out on the job.

The summary stopped at that point. Evidently, there were no further developments.

Just as I finished reading the file, the last reddish-gold arc of the sun disappeared on the horizon.

Lana slithered off a rock into the water.

"So what do you think?" I asked her. "Should I take the case?"

She popped her head above water-level and looked at me. Did I detect a gleam in her eye? Nah. Anyway, I knew that she knew it was already a foregone conclusion. The contessa, that wily fox, had known exactly how to pique my interest, how to reach into the depths of my soul. Whereas most people had an inner child there, I had something else: an inner vigilante. And it was ready to be set free.

CHAPTER 2

At nine the next morning, I pulled up in front of the squat, concrete-block building that housed the Central American Rescue Mission. The contessa's Rolls was already parked outside. I rang the bell and was buzzed in.

I was greeted by Coco snarling at my feet. The bitch obviously was not aware that I was highly trained in Krav Maga kicking skills, otherwise, she might have reconsidered. The contessa, though, seemed to read my thoughts, as usual, and commanded the dog to cease. Coco put her tail between her legs and scampered over to the contessa.

I could see the contessa was about to slap me with yet another reprimand about my new lack of social graces, so I cut her off. "Let's get to business. I have a contract here for you to sign."

"Very good," she said, and pulled out a pair of

reading glasses. She sat down and read over the terms of my services.

"Excellent," she said as she extracted a robin's-egg-blue Tiffany pen and signed the bottom line with a flourish.

I pulled out my leaky Harley pen with the flaming top that lit up in flashing red and gold, signed and handed her a copy.

"All right, now let me show you around," she said. "I think it would be useful for you to know a little more about the Rescue Mission and get acquainted with the people here." She waved around the room we were in. "This is our reception area."

The white plaster walls were covered with large, bright weavings depicting Central American village life.

"Our girls did those," the contessa said with pride. "We have a weekly women's group where they get together to make these and other traditional handicrafts, like woven handbags. We have a booth over at the flea market where we sell them."

I did a double-take. The Contessa von Phul in a flea market?

"Should I call you Contessa von Flea?" I asked, unable to control myself.

She pretended not to hear me. She gestured to a small weaving hanging on the wall. It showed a mother playing with an exuberant baby.

"Gladys did that one," she said.

I felt that pang again. Apparently Gladys had a fondness for children. I couldn't say the same about myself, but I did admire the trait in others. The weaving was meticulous, perfect to the finest detail. Not a thread was out of place. Clearly, Gladys took pride in her work.

I followed the contessa out of the reception area into a hallway as she chattered on about the mission.

"Of course, none of our boys and girls are here now, since they're working in the fields," the contessa said. "All our programs are in the evenings." She led me into a large room with chalkboard and desks. "This is our classroom. We have ESL teachers coming in every night of the week to teach English, all levels."

We walked down the hallway, which had several rooms off each side. "These are offices and meeting rooms. We have a part-time attorney on staff who helps the boys and girls with immigration. It's a real battle, but we've been able to get legal status for some of our clients. In fact, Gladys was one of them. Our lawyer got asylum for her just about a month before she was killed. Such a tragedy."

We continued down the hall. "We also have a part-time social worker. She does referrals and job placement. Often, our clients can get work permits while their immigration cases are pending, and then we can place them in jobs like housekeeping. It's a step up from working in the fields. That's what Gladys did. She was so motivated, the poor child."

We had reached the end of the hall. "And now I'd like to introduce you to our executive director."

She opened a door and I was hit with a blast of incense-filled air. Then, I found myself face-to-face with…Frida Kahlo.

Okay, so it wasn't really the late Mexican painter, it was just her double. She was a beautiful unibrowed woman in her fifties. Her dark brown eyes set off a broad nose and mouth. Her gray-streaked black hair was piled on top of her head in an elaborate braid intertwined with an emerald green ribbon. Emerald-and-gold chandelier earrings hung to her shoulders. Her white peasant blouse was embroidered at the neckline and sleeves, and her multicolored woven skirt hung gracefully to the floor.

"Harriet Horowitz, I'd like you to meet Dr. Guadalupe Lourdes Fatima Domingo," the contessa said.

I did another double take and glanced around the room. I'm half Catholic—the other half is Jewish—and I half expected the Virgin Mary to put in an appearance. She didn't.

"I'll be taking my leave now," the contessa said. "I have full faith in your ability to pursue this investigation. You will, of course, keep me posted."

"You betcha," I replied.

"Goodbye, then, both of you," she said, and went out the door.

Frida—I mean, the doctor—gave me a smile. "Just call me Lupe," she said. "How can I be of help?"

Taking out my flaming pen and my notepad, I said, "Why don't you begin by telling me all you know about Gladys?"

She reached into her desk, pulled out a photo and handed it to me.

"This is Gladys," she said softly.

I looked at the picture. It was a jarring contrast from the autopsy photos I'd looked at last night. The picture had been taken without Gladys's awareness. She was among a small group of women in conversation. Her dark eyes looked animated, her black hair shone brightly and her dark-red lips were open in a warm smile.

"She came to Florida about five years ago," Lupe said. "She was like many of the others from Guatemala. They come in small groups. They walk across the mountains into Mexico, then they slowly make their way across all of Mexico up to the Arizona border, where a coyote takes them over the border."

"A coyote?" I asked. "I didn't know they were domesticated."

"Not the animal," she said. "It's the common term for a smuggler."

"Oh," I said. Just stamp *dummy* across my forehead.

"They're the scum of the earth," she continued. "They cram these poor people into tractor trailers like cattle and sneak them across the border. Then they keep them loaded in there, waiting for other drivers to pick them up and bring them here to Florida. Invariably, a few die somewhere along the way. Imagine the heat in those trailers out there in the desert."

I had read about this kind of thing, but I'll admit I'd never given it a whole lot of thought. Well, remember that I've only been in recovery a few years. I *was* a Boca Babe most of my adult life, living in denial of the rest of the world. Yeah, I know, lame-ass excuse.

"Why do they take the risk?" I asked.

"These are indigenous people—Mayan Indians.

The governments in that region have always oppressed their basic human rights. Since the seventies,
there have been uprisings from the indigenous
people. You've heard of the *Zapatistas*, the *Chiapas?*"

I didn't want to betray my ex-Babe ignorance so I
just nodded. I don't think she was fooled.

"Basically, you have bloody civil strife that has
dragged on for decades. So when someone comes
along promising jobs in the U.S., it's a ticket to
paradise. Like many of them, Gladys wanted to earn
money to send back to her family. She had three
younger siblings back home. So she got here and
went to work in the fields. Some of the women there
got her involved with our agency. As the contessa
probably already told you, Gladys took English classes
here, and Judy, our lawyer, had just gotten her legal
asylum. Then just a couple weeks after that, a woman
called our employment service looking for a live-in
housekeeper, and Gladys was a perfect match. As you
can imagine, she was so excited to get out of the
fields."

As Lupe spoke, her gaze wandered off into some
unseen distance. Then she refocused on me. "And
that's all I can tell you about her. I'm sorry, I know
it's not much."

"Do you know who her friends were? Did she have a boyfriend?"

"She was close with one of our other clients, Eulalia. And she did have a boyfriend, Miguel."

"Well, those are two good places to start. How could I get in touch with them?"

"I'll be glad to take you to meet them up at the fields. Besides, you'll need an interpreter. They don't speak English very well."

"That'd be great," I said. "Also it'll give me a chance to see the scene of the crime."

"Okay," Lupe said. "How about I take you up there this afternoon? I'm just finishing writing a grant that I need to get out this morning. And I need to imbue it with good energy. So is one o'clock okay?"

"Great. I'll see myself out." As I stepped out the door, I saw her light another incense stick. I paused just outside the doorway, out of sight. Okay, so I was eavesdropping. It's an occupational hazard.

I heard an intonation emanate from within: "Command this fragrance strong and fast, to send out the spell that I cast."

Oh-kay. Weeeird.

I walked back down the hall and out the front door, got on my Hog, and roared away, reflecting on the case. After seeing the photos of Gladys alive and seeing what she left behind, she was real to me. A woman with a family, with hope, with so much potential and talent. Despite what the contessa had said about a part of me being a part of Gladys, I still wasn't sure what we had in common. An ex-Boca Babe and a Mayan illegal immigrant hardly inhabit the same worlds. But, by some twist of fate, our paths had intersected. Her journey down this road had ended. But mine was just beginning.

CHAPTER 3

I rode to my office, where I worked on another case for a couple hours—a scam involving a matchmaker who had failed to deliver the goods—then my stomach told me it was time for lunch. My encounter with Frida—I mean, Lupe—put my stomach in mind of Mexican food. The best I could do was Taco-to-Go. I chowed down on a gordita, bean burrito, beef taco and a Coke—damn, but a Corona would have hit the spot—then I rode back over to the Rescue Mission.

Lupe was ready to go and we got in her pickup truck. The cab, like her office, smelled of incense. A quartz crystal hung from the rearview mirror.

As we drove west to the tomato fields, I asked her how she'd gotten into her line of work.

"I grew up over in Immokalee," she said, referring to the small southwest Florida town that is the state's agricultural capital. "My parents were migrant farm workers from Mexico. We spent nine months of the year here in Florida, picking tomatoes, oranges, strawberries. In the summers, we went up to Maine for the cranberry harvest. Most migrant kids like me don't have a chance. Nobody outside their families gives a shit about them. They end up living the same life as their parents—'perpetuating the cycle of poverty,' as the politicos say—like it's all the kids' fault, right?"

I figured it was a rhetorical question so I didn't say anything and she went on.

"I was lucky. There was a young Anglo guy who came down from up north to organize the farm workers. He'd worked with César Chávez out in California. This was the late Sixties, so he was one of those revolutionaries who was going to change the world. I'm sure he's a stockbroker by now. Anyway, he put the idea in my head that I could actually go to college. So eventually I did—went to UF up in Gainesville, worked my way through. Of course, leaving my family was pretty tough, but they were behind me a hundred percent.

"So I majored in anthropology and then one of my professors started talking to me as if I could actually go to grad school, so I did that. Went to Harvard and got my Ph.D. in anthropology and linguistics. I did my fieldwork with the Mayans along the Mexican-

Guatemalan border, and learned several Mayan dialects along the way. Then I got a faculty job at Harvard, but a couple years later I came back down here for this job."

"Why'd you leave the ivory tower?" I asked.

"Trust me, *chica*, this job is so much more rewarding," she said. "I feel like I'm really helping my people, not just writing about them in the *Journal of Obscure Arcana* or whatever."

We drove on in silence for a while as I let her words sink in. We were entering farm country. Fields of green crops spread out around us. Massive sprinklers sprayed a fine mist over the land.

Something Lupe had said stuck in my brain.

"Wait a minute," I said. "You said you speak several Mayan dialects. Are you telling me these people don't speak Spanish?"

She laughed. "Yeah, that's a common misconception. They come from Latin America, they have Spanish names, they must speak Spanish, right? Wrong. Like I said earlier, these are indigenous people. They might know some Spanish if they went to school—of course, it's the official language, the 'legacy' of the *conquistadores*—but for the most part, they speak one of the native dialects."

"So when the police interviewed Gladys's friends through a Spanish interpreter, they might as well have been speaking Swahili?"

"That's about right. I tried to explain this to the cops, and offered to interpret, but they just brushed me off. Inspector Clueless tracks the Pink Panther. Stick with me, kid. We'll get Gladys's friends to tell us what they didn't tell the cops. It may take a while, but they'll tell us."

We had reached our destination, the tomato fields that were being harvested that day by a group of about twenty laborers, men and women. They were making their way up and down the rows of vines, picking off the still-green tomatoes from top to bottom and tossing them into baskets strapped to their backs as the hot Florida sun beat down on them. Man, what a way to make a living.

We got out of the truck and approached the workers.

"I see Miguel, Gladys's boyfriend," Lupe said, "but I don't see her friend Eulalia." She went over and began talking to one of the men. He shook his head and pushed past her as he continued his work. Lupe turned to some of the women. At that point the men glared at Lupe and the women, who cast fearful glances at us. Lupe motioned for us to head back to the truck.

"You need to understand something," she told me. "This is a very patriarchal culture. The men won't speak to us because it's beneath them, and the women are afraid of the men. You know, this is something we're working on at the Rescue Mission—trying to empower the women a little and trying to get the men to be less domineering—but it's an uphill battle, for sure. Not to mention they're all pretty wary of outsiders anyway, being mostly illegal and all. Even though they do know me, they still don't totally trust me. But, I do think we'll be able to get some information from Gladys's friends if we're persistent. Let's head over to the housing. Eulalia may be there."

We drove a mile or so until we reached a series of crumbling, tin-roofed wood shacks. We went into the first one. It was empty, except for rows of bunk beds. As we entered, a wall of heat hit me. Now, I don't have air-conditioning in my cabin, but at least I've got windows and there's a little breeze out there in the Glades. I didn't see any bath facilities, either. At least I've got a water supply and a septic tank with its own biodegradable treatment system. What did these people use—an outhouse?

"They live in here?" I asked.

Lupe nodded. "Company housing. Not exactly the Boca Raton Resort & Club, is it? Well, let's see if we can find Eulalia."

We proceeded through the row of shacks. All were empty of people until we reached the fifth one. There, we found two women, one lying on a bunk bed and the other sitting at the prone woman's side holding a wet cloth to her forehead.

"Eulalia," Lupe said.

The woman sitting looked up—I figured that was Eulalia—and Lupe asked her some questions. Eulalia glanced around nervously as Lupe spoke to her. The woman in the bed moaned. Her eyes were watery and unfocused, clear signs of fever.

There was a shuffling at the rear of the shack and a Mayan man came into view. He spoke to Eulalia. She cringed and turned away.

Lupe turned to me. "This is Eulalia. Her friend is obviously sick. She says they don't know what's wrong and she wants us to leave. She says it's happened before and her friend will be all right." Lupe sighed. "This is obviously not a good time to talk to Eulalia about Gladys. I'll come back here tomorrow to check on her and her friend. Let's go."

Just then, the door of the shack banged open, and a burly white man in overalls entered. He was tall, dark and seriously scary-looking. Beefy arms hung at his sides, culminating in a pair of massive hands that looked as if they could easily squeeze the life out of anyone who got in his way.

"It's Jake, the crew boss," Lupe whispered.

He curled back his upper lip, revealing a gold tooth that gleamed menacingly in the dim light of the shack.

"Now Ms. Domingo," he drawled with exaggerated politeness, "you know this is company property and you can't be coming around here without permission. So allow me to escort you off the premises."

"Take it easy, Jake," Lupe said. "We were just leaving."

He took a step forward and grabbed her by the hair. He pulled her head back, causing her to stumble and cry out in pain.

"What are you up to, you little wetback?" he growled. "And who's your little friend?" His eyes looked me up and down, settling on my boobs.

Well, this just wouldn't do. Nope, not at all. I reached into my boot and pulled my Magnum. I aimed it between his beady eyes and told him, "As Dirty Harry said, 'ask yourself one question: Do I feel lucky?'"

He held my gaze for a beat. Then he released Lupe and stepped aside to let us pass. I walked past him, my chin up and shoulders back. But I was shaking in my boots.

We climbed into Lupe's truck. She gave me a sideways glance and then we both burst out in nervous laughter.

Yee-oww! Move over, Dirty Harry—there's a new girl in town.

CHAPTER 4

We peeled away from the tomato fields, dust flying behind us. After we stopped laughing, I asked Lupe, "So, seriously, what's the deal with this crew boss?"

"It's like this," Lupe explained. "What you have here is modern-day slavery, indentured servitude. These people get lured to the U.S. with promises of jobs. Like I said earlier, a coyote takes them across the border. Somebody else trucks them to Florida, and they're put up in the company shacks. Then they're told they owe thousands of dollars for their smuggling, transportation and housing. They're put to work in the fields making a few bucks a day. You do the math—there's no way they'll ever be able to pay off the debt. Where the crew boss comes in, is intimidation. We've had people beaten, pistol-whipped, threatened with having their tongues cut out if they say anything to outsiders."

My inner vigilante was pounding on my chest wall, demanding to be let out. "This is outrageous!"

I exclaimed. "Slavery was outlawed in the nineteenth century! How can the government let this happen?"

Lupe smiled. "You know how it is, *chica*," she said. "Big Business pulls the strings. You think these tomato fields are little family farms? No way. You've heard of Big Tobacco? This is Big Tomato. Corporate America and its political campaign contributions. The human trafficking and debt bondage are done by contractors so the companies can wash their hands clean. And don't forget the buyers—do you know who one of the major purchasers of these tomatoes is? Taco-to-Go. Did you know they have a policy that they won't buy food from suppliers that mistreat animals, but they don't have any policy about mistreated humans? They've refused to even speak with the laborers about fair wages. So we're urging a public boycott of Taco-to-Go—our 'Toss the Taco' campaign. Say, have you had lunch?"

Oh, shit. How may poor Mayans had I just enslaved with that burrito and taco? If knocking off my husband didn't send me straight to hell, this would do it for sure.

"Uh, yeah, I ate," I mumbled.

I was spared further elaboration by our arrival back at the Rescue Mission. "I'll tell you what," Lupe said.

"Why don't you come here tomorrow night? That's when we have the women's handicrafts group. Eulalia is usually there. She may be more willing to talk to you without the men around."

I agreed. We said our goodbyes and I donned my leathers and helmet and mounted my bike. I was a little beat from the day's battles. After all, I'd warded off Coco, the contessa and the crew boss, all in a day's work. Yep, I was ready to hit the Hennessy. Unfortunately, I still had one more battle to face that day— grocery shopping at Publix.

If you think I exaggerate, you haven't shopped in South Florida. The war zone begins in the parking lot. Between the phone-jabbering soccer moms in their SUVs—Stupid User Vehicles—and the geriatric set in their Jags and jitneys, you can consider yourself damn lucky if you manage to park without engaging in hand-to-hand combat. And if you think it's tough in a four-wheeled vehicle, imagine yourself on a two-wheeler. Granted, when riding a bike you have to assume that the entire driving populace is blind and act accordingly, but are they deaf, too? You can hear a Hog coming from a mile away. But not around here, apparently.

The situation is no different inside the store, only

the weaponry. Now armed with their shopping carts, the combatants charge down the aisles, ramming anything in their way.

I was among the victors that day, ending up in express checkout with only a twisted ankle resulting from a failed escape maneuver in the ethnic foods aisle, where I snagged some matzo ball soup in place of the salsa that my conscience compelled me to scratch off my list. I have to admit, this hassle of grocery shopping, and having to actually prepare my own food, made me long for my former life. As a Boca Babe, the only thing I'd ever made for dinner was reservations or delivery calls.

As I waited there in the endless (did I say *express?*) lane, my eye glanced upon a women's magazine cover promising me a "Better Butt By Summer!" Yeah, right. It had taken me years to develop buns of steel. And even so, I still had some cellulite hanging on for dear life.

I finally reached the cashier. In keeping with the battle theme, she was in full war paint. Her foundation would have served well in a housing development, her eyelashes could have swept the floor and the contrast between her lip liner and lipstick gave new meaning to the term *chiaroscuro*. Even Tammy Faye Bakker would have run for cover.

Just as I decided that she must be a drag queen and was searching for beard stubble underneath that spackle, she flashed me an angelic smile and said, "You have beautiful eyes." And here I had been having these uncharitable thoughts about her/him. Yep, I was hell-bound, no two ways about it.

But, then again, I am cursed with a double dose of guilt. With a Catholic mother and a succession of Jewish fathers, how could it be otherwise?

My birth father, Harold Horowitz, traveling salesman extraordinaire, died when I was still a baby, as a result of a freak equine-bovine encounter. That is to say, his '67 Mustang hit a Texas longhorn up near Frostproof, Florida. That's right. Dad was a Jewish Willie Loman.

My mother, Stella Celeste Kucharski Horowitz Fleischer Steinblum Fishbein Rosenberg, is a Botox Babe. Where did you think I got it from? Babeness is a hereditary disease. As you may have surmised, Mom is a repeat matrimonial offender. She finally found wedded bliss, in addition to economic ecstasy, with husband no. 5, Mortimer Rosenberg. (Or was it Rosenbaum? Rosenblum? Rosencrantz? Shit, I can never remember.) Mort got his start in the family funeral business up in New York, and his fortune grew when he expanded the enterprise on the heels of the Great Jewish Exodus—no, not the one from Egypt to the Promised Land—the one from New York to Florida. He really hit the big time with his Value-Added Mortuary Package (VAMP, also known as casket-in-a-basket)—casket, flowers, rabbi rental, all for $1,999.99. Mort's Mortuaries now line the Florida coast from Miami to Daytona Beach.

Mort himself went to rest in the big funeral parlor in the sky a couple years ago, and Mom hasn't remarried. Yet. Right now she was on a two-week cruise of the Greater and Lesser Antilles, sponsored by the International Spy Museum of Washington, D.C. Ostensibly, this was one of those life-long learning deals for seniors where they were to attend a lecture series by prominent experts on Cold War espionage. But I wondered about her true motives for going. The male-to-female ratio for her age group was bound to be tipped in her favor on a cruise like this, as opposed to what it was in Boca. So I was seriously hoping that this wasn't in fact a ploy by Mom to meet Mr. Right Version 6.0 on board and elope. That's all I needed in my life—some Secret Agent 007 type with an untraceable past to marry Mom's money. Not that I wanted her money for myself, you understand. It's just that, how would it look for the owner of ScamBusters' own mother to be scammed?

I hurried out of the grocery store. I was just backing my bike out of the parking space when suddenly there was a screech of metal up ahead as a Caddy backed into an Olds waiting to take its place. This set off a succession of car horns.

It was then that it struck me that I really didn't have to worry about going to hell, because I was already there.

I finally reached home. As I pulled up to my cabin, I felt another pang of longing for the past. As a Boca Babe, my idea of a perfect house had been 10,000 square feet with no kitchen. Now here I was in lodgings the size of a matchbox. But at least there were no boxing matches going on in here.

My mind wandered back to those days. The worst thing about the beatings was that they had been so unpredictable. It may seem weird, but at least if you know when you're going to get the shit beat out of you, you can be prepared—emotionally, anyway—and relax in the meantime. But it doesn't work that way in real life. So I was constantly on alert, hyper-vigilant. I couldn't let my guard down for a second. Always trying to be on good behavior to prevent another attack. But the definition of "good behavior" kept changing. Something that pleased Bruce one day would piss him off the next. Like the way I interacted with his clients at social events. One week it was, "Harriet, I'm so proud of you. They all loved you. You're smart and funny and beautiful. I wouldn't be where I am without you." The next week it was, "What the hell were you doing, trying to upstage me in front of my clients? You'd better remember who brings in the bucks here. You think I married you for your brains? If I wanted your opinion, I'd give it to you."

Then the hitting would start. One time, he shoved me and I went down, hitting my skull on the edge of the dining room table. A platter of hot seafood étouffée came down on me, scalding my arm.

"Clean it up!" he yelled, kicking me as I tried to rise.

So that's how it went, week in, week out. It took me years to figure out I was trying to control something I couldn't.

I forced my mind back to the present. What a day. I needed to unwind, to chill, to restore my Zen-like state. Of course, there was only one way to do that: motorcycle maintenance. I had taken some basic classes back when I first got my bike. As a former Boca Babe, I couldn't tell a shifting fork from a salad fork, a cylinder block from a cinder block. But I did have a desire to learn, plus a major drive to depend on no one but myself.

I pulled the Hog off the airboat and onto the porch. I muscled it up onto its center stand and then unscrewed the oil filler cap. The oil level was just about a quart down, so I topped it off. I changed the transmission fluid and adjusted the drive belt. By then, I was on my way to getting as tranquil as I ever get.

I sat down with my Hennessy. Lana was splayed out on a nearby rock, soaking up the last rays of the day. I reflected on what I'd learned about the Mayan slaves—the injustice, the exploitation, the greed.

"It's a cruel world," I said to Lana. Her only response was to snap at a turtle that swam by.

CHAPTER 5

The following morning I decided to contact Tricia Weinstein, the woman who had employed Gladys as a housekeeper. According to the police report, she was an estate attorney with a prominent law firm in town. I was able to reach her at work, though not without some wrangling with her receptionist. After I explained the reason for my call and asked to meet with her, she stated that she was extremely busy but could see me for a short time that afternoon at two.

I spent the morning at my office, tracking down a client's missing funds to an account in the Turks and Caicos. At two I walked into the law offices of Weinstein, Weinberg & Weintraub in downtown Boca. Gold-and-black lettering on the entrance door proclaimed, "Visit us on the web at www.www.com." Puh-leeze.

The receptionist was a Boca Babe wannabe. Here's how you tell the Boca Babe aspirants from the arrivals: It's not a matter of artificial versus authentic, it's the quality of the artifice. The wannabes' bleached blond hair has dark roots and split ends, their artificial nails are press-on rather than silk wrap and their make-up is sparkly rather than subtle. But the fake boobs are the same.

She did the head-to-toe body scan. I had on my usual all-black, all-stretch attire and sported my usual hair, makeup and nail job—that is to say, none. She eyed me disdainfully.

I handed her my card. "Harriet Horowitz to see Tricia Weinstein," I said.

She eyed me with a mix of what I could gather only as curiosity and suspicion, then pushed a button on her phone console and spoke into her headset.

"Ms. Weinstein will be with you soon. Please have a seat," she said in a snippy tone as if I were a nuisance.

It couldn't be soon enough as far as I was concerned.

I sat down on one of the couches opposite her desk and looked around the room. It was a far cry from yesterday's reception area in the Rescue Mission. The decor was classic Boca: Art Nouveau Riche. A Persian rug covered the floor, the walls were hung with original oils and the furnishings were leather and mahogany. If the decorators had stopped there it would have been okay, but they had to screw it up by adding on: faux Roman statuary, faux Ming vases and English chintz draperies. Suffice it to say, Boca style does not involve understated elegance.

The receptionist broke into my design critique. "Excuse me, ma'am, Ms. Weinstein will see you now. Follow me."

She led me into an inner office.

The first thing my keen powers of detection picked up about Tricia Weinstein was that she was pregnant. About eight months. Yeah, okay—so it was pretty obvious. The second thing was that she was perfect. Her dark brown hair hung about her shoulders in a perfect flip, her bright blue eyes and delicate nose were flawless, her aqua-blue maternity suit could only have been couture and her French manicure was worthy of Marie Antoinette. Not that I was envious or anything.

The perfection extended to her office. Sleek filing cabinets lined the far wall. Folders were neatly stacked on her desk. There wasn't a paper clip or a pencil out of place.

She extended a hand. "It's a pleasure to meet you,

Ms. Horowitz," she said. "I'm glad someone is following up on Gladys's case. It's a travesty that the police haven't been able to solve it. But I don't know what help I can be. I already told the police everything I know."

"Well, if you wouldn't mind repeating it, I would appreciate that. It's always possible that you might remember some new detail. And I prefer to hear things for myself, rather than just read about it in the police report."

She glanced at her Rolex. "All right. But I really don't have much time. I've got a client coming soon, and I'm trying to wrap up a lot of work here before I go on maternity leave in a few weeks."

"I'll be as brief as possible," I lied. "Can you tell me how you came to employ Gladys?"

"Well, I needed a housekeeper. I had gone to some fund-raising event for Contessa von Phul's charity a few months before and I learned that the Rescue Mission had this employment service, so I called to see if they might have anyone available. They sent a few women for me to interview, and I selected Gladys."

"And how did she work out for you?"

"Great. She did her tasks just as I wanted, was no

trouble at all. I've been told I'm a perfectionist and that I'm not easy to work for. But Gladys and I got along fine. She was very reliable. Until she disappeared, that is."

Yeah, I guess getting killed might make you a little unreliable.

She seemed to realize her faux pas. "Oh, I didn't mean that like it sounded. Of course, she didn't disappear intentionally, the poor thing. But that's what I thought at the time."

"Tell me about that day."

"Well, there's not much to tell. The evening before she disappeared, Gladys said she was going to her English class. My husband and I went out and we didn't check on her when we came back late that night. I just assumed she was in her room. But the next morning, she didn't come down at her usual time for breakfast. I knocked on her door and when she didn't answer, I went in and she wasn't there. I didn't report her missing because, like I said, I just assumed she had bailed out on the job. I called the Rescue Mission to complain, but they assured me that it wasn't like her and that all their workers were very reliable. They were so apologetic, I decided to give them another try, so when Gladys still hadn't

MIRIAM AUERBACH   59

shown up a couple days later, I hired another house-keeper from them—Adriana. She's still with us. And a couple days after that, they found Gladys's body and called me."

Just then the phone on her desk rang. She picked it up, listened for a moment and then looked up at me. "I'm terribly sorry," she said. "I must take this call. It's very important. And as I said, I have another client coming soon. Anyway, I don't see how I can be of further help. I've told you just about all I know. Gladys only worked for me for a couple weeks before she disappeared."

"That's okay," I said, even though I sensed I was getting the brush-off. "Can we meet another time? I'd like to ask you about Gladys's personality, her friends, that kind of thing. It shouldn't take long."

"Oh, all right," she sighed, and opened a large day planner on her desk. She flipped through the pages that were full of bulleted items. Man, that woman was busy—and organized. It looked as if just about every hour of every day was filled with something.

"I can fit you in Saturday morning at my house," she pronounced. "Here is the address." She jotted it down on a notepad and handed the sheet to me. Then she pushed a button on her phone.

"Hello, Mr. Finkel," she said. "Yes, your will is ready. That's right, your wife gets what's stipulated in the prenup, your first wife gets nothing…. What's that? Your older son has shacked up with a shipper from Bahrain? Oh, a stripper from Ukraine. Right… Your younger son hit on your wife? Well, he is about her age…. No, I said that's an outrage! Strike both your sons from the will? No problem. We'll have it ready for you in the morning."

I'd heard enough. Enough to deduce that Tricia Weinstein's client was a member of the TWTW Club—Trolls With Trophy Wives. Boca's overrun with them. But they were the least of my worries at the moment. Unless one of them was the killer.

CHAPTER 6

I called the contessa to update her on my progress. Then I had a few hours to spare before going to the Rescue Mission to try to speak with Eulalia, so I decided to take a ride out to the beach. I rode to A1A, the road that runs parallel to the Atlantic Ocean, then headed north. It was a day straight out of paradise. February is one of the best months in South Florida. It was sunny and the temperature hovered around seventy. There was a breeze coming in off the ocean that blended with the wind resistance buffeting me as the Hog chugged up the road. For all my bitching about Boca, this is why I stay here—it's just damn gorgeous. I took it nice and slow, putting along, looking at the breakers come into shore and looking at the people looking at me and the bike.

Most people don't know quite what to make of a woman riding her own bike. A woman in control of a rumbling, throbbing machine that might be five times her own weight. Most people don't know what to make of bikers in general, for that matter. The uninformed masses think we're all a bunch of drugged-out, sex-crazed, bullying outlaws.

But I love riding because of the freedom, the noise, the wind and the speed. I feel in control, and that's beautiful.

That afternoon, I rode all the way up to Palm Beach, then turned around and did it all over again in reverse, then headed inland to the Rescue Mission. Lupe greeted me at the door. Today she had on shades of bright red and yellow, with oversize gold and ruby jewelry to match.

"C'mon in," she said. "The women are in back. Eulalia is there."

We went down the hall into one of the back rooms. Eight Mayan women were seated in a circle, weaving tapestries. Kind of an Oppressed Women's Quilting Circle. But wow, were they different away from the men and the tomato fields. The fearful looks and the cringing, defensive stances were gone, replaced with talking and laughter.

Then I had to come in and ruin all that. When Lupe called her name, Eulalia got that deer-in-the-headlights look. Lupe walked over and put her arm around her and spoke to her softly. Eulalia got up and the three of us went into another room.

Lupe told me, "I've explained to her who you are and that you're not going to hurt her in any way. I've told her you're not with the government or anything like that, that you just want to try to find Gladys's killer, and you'll keep everything she tells you in confidence. Okay, go ahead and ask your questions."

I smiled at Eulalia. She was a small woman with dark eyes, golden-brown skin, high cheekbones, a broad nose and the same dark red lips as Gladys. I felt a sudden urge to protect Eulalia, as if in some way that could atone for Gladys's brutal murder.

She sat with her hands folded in her lap, keeping her eyes downcast, occasionally casting fleeting glances upward through a fringe of black bangs. I spoke directly to her, rather than to Lupe.

"Can you tell me about your relationship with Gladys?" I asked. Lupe translated.

Eulalia looked warily from me to Lupe. Lupe gave her an encouraging smile.

"We grew up together in our village. We came here together, worked together, did everything together." Lupe translated Eulalia's words verbatim, as only a trained interpreter would know how to do. Eulalia began to sob. Lupe held her hand.

"Tell me about the day she disappeared."

"She had come here to our English class that night. Then she went back to that house she lived in and I went back to the fields. I never saw her again." Eulalia's shoulders shook as she cried uncontrollably now. I paused to let it pass.

"That night, did Gladys say she was concerned about anything? Did she seem worried at all?"

"No. She was very happy. She talked about how wonderful her new job was compared to working in the fields. She really wanted me to get my legal papers, too, so I could do what she was doing. The lawyer here is still working on my case."

"Did Gladys ever talk about any problems with her boyfriend Miguel?"

Eulalia looked up at Lupe, then quickly cast her eyes downward again. "No," she said.

Her actions belied her words. But I didn't want to push her for fear it would shut her off to me completely. I let it drop, for now.

I'd about run out of questions, too. There sure wasn't much to grasp on to here.

"Do you have any ideas about who might have wanted Gladys dead?" I asked.

"No, no," Eulalia cried, looking up at me.

I put my hand on her back. "Thank you," I said. "You've been very helpful. Don't worry, I won't tell anyone that you talked to me. And I promise, I won't give up on Gladys."

Eulalia got up to go. She walked to the door and put her hand on the knob. Then she stopped. Lupe opened her mouth to say something and I quickly put up my hand and shook my head at her. As a P.I., just like a therapist, I had seen this behavior many times: the Doorknob Confession. People who denied having anything to say throughout an interview suddenly opened up just as the session came to a close. I knew we had to let whatever it was Eulalia wanted us to know to come out without interruption.

And it did.

She reached beneath the waistband of her skirt and pulled out a crinkled, dirty, legal-size envelope and handed it to me. She whispered something.

"Gladys gave this to me a few days before she disappeared," Lupe translated. Then Eulalia looked me right in the eyes and spoke directly to me. In English.

"Please, please help me. Help us." Then she quickly shuffled out the door, closing it behind her.

Lupe and I stared at each other, wide-eyed and slack-jawed. What did she mean, "Help me, help us?" Was she, or were the other Mayan women, in danger? Was Gladys's murder part of some larger peril?

I looked down at the envelope in my hands. I opened it and pulled out two torn, dirty sheets of paper. Lupe and I bent over eagerly to read them. The first was some kind of ledger sheet, handwritten in Spanish. I picked up the word *Guatemala*, the name of Miguel, and some dates going back a year to a year and a half ago. I looked questioningly at Lupe.

She reached into her cleavage and pulled out the coolest pair of reading glasses I'd ever seen—sleek, multicolored frames attached to a beaded necklace around her neck. Of course, I should have expected no less from Frida Kahlo's doppelgänger.

"It's some kind of shipments to Guatemala," she said. "See these dates? And these numbers? It's showing quantities, but it doesn't say quantities of what."

"What's this?" I pointed to some letters beneath Miguel's name: FLGI.

"I have no idea."

"Could this be Gladys's writing?" I asked. "In Spanish?"

"Yes, it's possible. Gladys may have known how to write some Spanish. Mayan languages are primarily oral, so if Mayans do learn to write, it's usually in Spanish."

I looked at the other sheet of paper. It appeared to be part of a medical chart. The top read "Isis Comprehensive Women's Health and Fertility Clinic," followed by an address in a fashionable Boca neighborhood. The left margin was torn off, but what remained read "UD," followed by Gladys's name.

"Any idea what this is?" I asked Lupe.

"None," she replied. "Let me go talk to Eulalia alone for a minute."

She went out and I was left to gaze around the room. God, don't you hate it when you're left alone and there's nothing around to snoop into, to satisfy your curiosity, your nosiness?

In the vacuum, Britney Spears's cover of the Stones' "(I Can't Get No) Satisfaction" started to run through my mind. Yeah, I know, musical sacrilege. So sue me.

Just then Lupe returned.

"Eulalia insists she doesn't know what these papers

mean," she said. "She says Gladys gave them to her without explaining what they were, she just asked her to hang on to them. Eulalia says she always carried the envelope on her because she didn't trust leaving it at the shacks while she was out. I asked her why she hadn't said anything about this when the police questioned her, and she said she was afraid. Well, that's totally understandable. Of course, they're all afraid of being deported, or worse. But she thought she could trust you." Lupe said this with a wry expression.

I feigned offense. "As well she can," I huffed. "I am the Diva of Discretion. Well, I think it's time to pay a friendly visit to Miguel. You game?"

"Are you kidding? You're lookin' at one game dame, lady."

And so the game was on.

CHAPTER 7

Night had fallen by the time Lupe and I drove out in her truck to the tomato fields. The temperature had dropped a few degrees and the stars were out. We drove in companionable silence. Eulalia's plaintive appeal—"Help me, help us"—echoed in my mind until we pulled up to the workers' shacks.

A few men were sitting around outside, drinking from a bottle in a paper bag. We approached and Lupe asked them (so I gathered) where we might find Miguel. The men hooted and hollered, presumably calling for Miguel to come out of the shacks. The door of one of the buildings opened, and Miguel emerged. He was a small, wiry guy in his twenties. His black hair and clothes were disheveled, and his deep-set dark eyes bore a bewildered look.

"Can we go somewhere to talk?" I asked, and Lupe translated for him. He turned his head back and forth between us and his "boyz," like a spectator in a tennis match. His male pride won out. He squared his shoulders, thrust out his chin and declared (as Lupe translated), "I don't talk to women."

"Is that so?" I said. "Then I guess you'd rather talk to the police."

He went through the tennis-spectator thing again. Trouble was, we weren't exactly at Boca Bath & Tennis, and our score wasn't exactly love-love, either. My patience was running out. Finally he turned his back on his homeys and walked to us. The three of us walked farther out into the tomato fields. More hoots and howls followed. We proceeded through the rows of tomato vines till we were well away from the shacks. There we found some wooden packing crates and our little trio sat down for a cozy chat.

"Miguel," I explained as Lupe translated, "I am investigating the murder of Gladys. I know you were her boyfriend. So of course you're the prime suspect. The police know that, too. I have some new information that links you to her death." It was a slight bluff, a common trick of the trade. "So, I think it would be in your best interest to tell me what you know about her murder."

He crossed his arms over his skinny chest and glared at us with his narrow black eyes. "I don't know anything about it. I already told that to the police," he told Lupe.

A smug smile crept on to his face. That was a mistake. The little prick was rapidly getting on my nerves. If he'd really cared for Gladys, where did he get off with this macho attitude, or whatever the equivalent term was in their language?

I pulled out the ledger sheet of shipments to Guatemala. "What's this?" I asked.

I detected a flicker of fear and uncertainty in those belligerent eyes. Then it passed. "Where did you get that?" he yelled, grabbing for the paper. I snapped it back out of his reach.

"I'm asking the questions here." Of course I wasn't going to reveal my source.

He did the arm-folding and jaw-jutting again. "I don't know what it is. I don't know what you're talking about, you crazy woman. And if the police ask, I'll tell them the same thing."

That did it. "Listen, you bottom-feeding pond scum dirtbag," I said. "You spill the beans or I'll spill your guts all over this godforsaken field."

"Um, Harriet?" said Lupe. "That's not really going to, like, translate."

Well, hell. My Dirty Harry act would be lost in

translation. Well, there was only one fix for that: I had to resort to a universal language, a *lingua franca*. I reached out, grabbed his crotch, and squeezed.

He screamed and snatched for my arm. But Lupe was quicker. She seized his wrists, then twisted his arms behind his back. I looked at her in awe. Damn! We made a hell of team.

I turned back to Miguel. His eyes bulged.

"Now, you were saying?" I asked as I casually inspected the chewed nails on my other hand.

"I don't know what it is," he repeated, but this time his voice sounded as if he'd just taken a toke and was trying to speak without exhaling.

Gosh, my attempt at smoothing the flow of cross-cultural communication was falling a little short. I screwed the nuts and bolts a little tighter.

"Say, Lupe," I remarked. "Have you ever tried those hand-grip exercises? You know, with those spring-loaded resistance gizmos? Look like the clamps on a pair of jumper cables? You oughtta try 'em. They really increase your grip strength."

She rolled her eyes.

"Yeah, I know," I said. "Not gonna translate."

I turned back to Miguel. "So you're sure you've never seen this piece of paper before?"

This time his voice came out in a falsetto. "It's a shipment record. Gladys kept the records because she could write and add."

"Well, isn't that interesting. Just what kind of shipments are we talking about, Miguel?"

He didn't respond, so I ratcheted the pressure up a notch.

"Food," he squeaked. "Tomatoes, oranges. For the people back home. They're starving back there."

"Well, how humanitarian of you. And what's this?" With my free hand I pointed to the letters— FLGI—beneath his name on the ledger sheet. "Some kind of UN relief agency?"

More pressure, more squeaking. Lupe prefaced her translation, "It's Spanish. An acronym. *La Frente por la Liberación de la Gente Indígene*, the Indigenous People's Liberation Front." She went on in Miguel's own words. "It's a small group of us here, trying to help our brothers back home."

Beads of sweat were starting to trickle down his face. I figured I couldn't squeeze any more out of him without him passing out, and then what use would he be? I let go. Lupe followed. He fell to the ground, writhing and moaning.

"Thank you ever so much for your time," I said

sweetly. "You've been such a help. I tell you, just when I start to despair of the human race, a ray of sunshine like you comes along to restore my faith. Well, we'll be going now. You stay in touch, ya hear?"

We reached Lupe's truck without any trouble and started our drive along the dusty road out of the fields.

"Okay," I said, "So we've got some kind of renegade exile group here supporting the freedom fighters back in the old country. Sending food, ostensibly. So what's the big deal? Is Big Tomato upset about employee pilferage? Worried about a few tomatoes getting diverted from their destiny with Taco-to-Go? There's some missing pieces here, Lupe. I don't totally buy Miguel's story."

"I'm with you, *chica*," she said.

Just then we passed by a large concrete warehouse that was located away from the workers' living quarters. A few Mayan men were standing outside. As we drove by, they stopped talking to turn and watch us. I could see their faces reflected in the sideview mirror, the red glow of our taillights making them look like jack-o'-lanterns. They looked wary.

"Lupe," I said. "Keep on trucking. Don't let on that anything's up. But let's pull off a couple miles up ahead. I want to go back and do some reconnaissance on those boys. I'd like to know what's in that building that they seem so protective of."

We pulled off the road and into some tall grasses that surrounded the truck, blocking it from view from the road.

"Okay, I'm off," I said to Lupe. "You don't mind waiting?"

"No way, José. I haven't had this much fun since Father Hidalgo and the Holy Ghosts came through here with their unsanctioned tent revival a couple years ago. Go on, girl, I'm not going anywhere."

I took off into the darkness.

CHAPTER 8

I hiked along the edge of the dirt road, ready to dive for cover in the tall grasses at the first sign of anyone approaching. The air was still and I had only the crickets for company. They leapt up in front of me, as if to guide my path. Or block it.

Up ahead, I saw the building where the men had been gathered. They were no longer standing there, but a faint light shone from inside. I stepped off the road and into the tomato field. I got down on my hands and knees so that I would be hidden by the vines, and crawled up to the back of the building. There was a small window about seven feet up. I looked around for something to boost me up. I found a packing crate, turned it on its side, climbed up and slowly raised myself to the window.

Peering inside, I saw the group of Mayan men. They were packing tomatoes into crates, then loading the crates onto a tarp-covered pickup truck. Except along with the tomatoes, they were packing something else—ammo. They were disassembling a collection of guns, as well as some hand grenades and what looked like a couple of land mines. They were putting a layer of tomatoes in each crate, followed by a layer of weapons and topped with another tomato layer.

Well, I guess that would make for some pretty fiery chili at Taco-to-Go. Yep, I could see the menu items now. Today's Specials: Bullets 'n' Burritos. Grenades 'n' Guacamole.

Suddenly I felt something crawling up my right pants leg. Oh, shit! Some creepy crawly insect or slug or whatever. My whole body shuddered. I swatted at my leg, then balanced on the crate with my left leg and spasmodically shook my right.

Well, you can guess what happened. The crate and I came crashing down with a resounding thud. Immediately there was commotion and noise inside the building.

Damn! It would take them a few seconds to get out the door and around to the back of the building. I looked around frantically for a hiding place. I spotted an old porcelain tub by the side of the building, covered with a wooden lid. I rushed over, shoved aside the lid, climbed in, and wrestled the lid back over me just as pounding footsteps and voices came around the corner.

I lay there, holding my breath. Well, at least I'd gotten rid of the bug. Except—wait—now I had another problem. What had I gotten myself into? Oh, shit squared! I was lying in a vat of rotten tomatoes!

The ripe juices oozed all over me, seeping into the seams of my clothes right down to my thong underwear. I was a human stew. And I was trapped.

I lay there, helpless, until the footsteps and voices faded into the distance. Then I lay there some more till I was sure they had gone.

Finally, I climbed out, dripping tomato sauce. I started the hike back to Lupe's truck. There I was, walking down the dusty, deserted road—a biker chick cacciatore. Just sprinkle some oregano on me, bake for an hour and serve with *rotini al dente*.

At last I reached the truck. Lupe was standing in front of it, barefoot, legs spread wide, arms reaching toward the sky, face turned toward the moonlight. I hated to interrupt what looked like a private moment, but I sure as hell wasn't going to stand around and marinate.

I cleared my throat. Lupe came out of her trance and ran toward me.

"What took you so long?" she said frantically. "I was about to call my brothers for backup."

"Your brothers?"

"Yeah, Balthasar, Gaspar and Melchior."

I blinked. "The Three Wise Men?"

"Yeah, *Mamá* and *Papá* were a little devout, if you haven't guessed already. But never mind that now. Holy shit! What the hell happened to you?"

"Let's move," I said. "I'll tell you on the way."

CHAPTER 9

It was the wee hours of the morning when I finally reached my cabin. I stood on the porch, peeled off my clothes and dropped them right there. I'd have to take them to the laundromat in the morning. I went straight into the shower, where I stood till the hot water ran out. Then it was back to the porch with my Hennessy.

Lana was nowhere in sight. She must have been snug in her gator bed, like the rest of the sane world. I drained my Hennessy and turned in.

When I woke up, it was almost noon. With yesterday's starring role in *Revenge of the Rotten Tomatoes*, I wasn't operating at peak performance. On top of that, last night had been one of my Nightmare Nights. I get them every couple months or so—replays of my marriage, from the beatings and put-downs to the final showdown at the Shapiro wedding shindig. That last part plays out in slo-mo.

We're at the reception, sitting at a big round table

with four other couples, all friends from the country club. It's a formal affair, and the setting is beautiful, with soft lights and flowers everywhere. The bride and groom are young and attractive. They're in love, happy and confident of their future. Like Bruce and I once were. I've downed a couple glasses of champagne and I have a warm feeling inside. I start to think, maybe Bruce and I can be that way again. If we both just try…a love like ours doesn't just die, does it?

Bruce is talking to the woman on his other side. I reach for his hand, wanting to connect, to let him know I still love him and want him.

He pushes my hand away.

"Don't interrupt me," he snaps.

My heart sinks, my whole insides just collapse. Tears start streaming down my face.

"Oh, come off it with the hurt act," he says. "Poor baby," he mocks me.

He stands abruptly, knocking his chair backward to the floor. The table goes silent, all eyes on us. I can't believe it. He's never acted like this in public, in front of our friends.

"Now look what you made me do," he yells.

"Hey, Bruce, take it easy," somebody says. But

Bruce doesn't listen. He pushes me and I go tumbling back in my own chair.

In that moment I know that's it. Our relationship will never be like it once was. His abuse will just go on and on. And no one will stop it. Except me. The love is dead. And so is the hope. I can't live this way anymore.

People have gotten up from their seats and are moving toward us, but my vision narrows and they recede into blackness at the edges. I see Bruce's tuxedo jacket on the back of his chair, on the floor next to me. I know his gun is in the jacket pocket. He's gotten really paranoid lately, he's been carrying it everywhere.

I sit up on the floor, reach into the pocket, grab the gun and point it at him with both hands.

"Go ahead, make my day," I say.

He lunges at me, fist raised.

There's a blast. My arms fly up and over my head. My torso slams backward on the floor.

I can't hear anything. But my vision starts to expand. I see blood spattered everywhere. I see our tablemates, petrified, horrified.

Then my hearing returns, and I hear their screams. And then I hear my own.

I wake, still screaming.

So now you know my deep dark secret. I'm not as unfazed by the killing as I make out. Truth be known, after the big face-off, I just went balls to the wall hurtling into my new life.

But on these Nightmare Nights, the past haunts me. You really can't just get over having killed someone. So for all my tough exterior, there's a tormented interior. I remind myself that, ultimately, it was him or me. If I wasn't Dirty Harriet now, I'd be Dead Harriet. Maybe the fatal blow wasn't coming right then and there, but it was on its way.

But I couldn't think about all that now. I employed my usual coping strategy—suppressing it all to the most remote corner of my mind. I fixed myself a hearty brunch of bacon-and-cheese omelet and hash browns. Yeah, I know, cholesterol city. My arteries would just have to deal with it. As for my cellulite, it wasn't going anywhere anyway, so what the hell. One of the things I didn't miss about my former life was the constant dieting in order to maintain the perfect bod. As a Boca Babe, some of my friends had snorted NutraSweet because they thought it was diet coke.

Just as I took the last bite, my phone rang.

"Harriet, how are you, dear?"

Oh, no—Mom! Just what I needed right now.

Don't get me wrong. I love my mother. But I loathe her. But I know that someday my mother won't be around to chap my ass anymore, and then I'll be Seriously Alone. But she always calls at the most inconvenient times. But she calls because she cares. But…

Okay, so maybe you've gathered that my relationship with my mother is…ambivalent. As a Botox Babe who raised me to follow in her Manolo-clad footsteps, she, of course, represents everything I've turned my back on. And she, of course, takes that personally.

The thing is, it took me till my thirties to go through my teenage rebellion phase. I haven't grown out of it yet—and don't intend to—so Mom and I are locked in what looks to be a perpetual battle of the wills. During my marriage, I had carefully kept my domestic abuse secret from her, and she's never quite gotten over my blowing away her "perfect" son-in-law. She has, however, accepted the fact that he's gone, and therefore, the only logical conclusion is that I need to get a replacement. And in her view, my A & A—Appearance and Attitude—aren't going to cut it. So she's forever on my case for me to change my hair, my clothes, my ideas…basically myself, that's all.

"Harriet! Are you there?"

I took a deep breath, determined to do my best to avert a long-distance confrontation.

"Yes! I'm fine, Mom," I said. "How's the *Merry Mermaid?*" That was the cruise ship she was on, attending those lectures on Cold War espionage in between snacking, sunning, drinking, shuffleboard and whatever else it is people do on those things.

"It's wonderful," she replied. "The things I am learning about! Underground tunnels, dead drops, reconnaissance missions. And all the tools of the trade—lipstick pistols, buttonhole cameras, shoe transmitters. It's fascinating!"

"And how are the islands?"

"Absolutely beautiful. We stopped at Saint Vincent today, tomorrow it's on to Saint Lucia, then Saint Kitts."

"So it's the All Saints Spy Tour," I said. "Cool."

At least she hadn't mentioned anything about meeting some mysterious man on board. I almost asked, but then stopped myself. Did I really want to go there?

"And what's new with you?" she asked.

"Well, I've got a new case. A murder, actually—"

"A murder!" she said, cutting me off. "Oh, Harriet, that is so unseemly. Don't you think it's time for you to stop this private investigator silliness and move on with your life? You're not getting any younger, you know. You need a man to take care of you, and you're not going to find him in that swamp you call a home!"

I took a deep breath, but it did no good.

"I have moved on with my life," I snapped. "And I intend to stay a single swamp-dwelling ScamBuster!"

"I only say this because I love you," she managed to say before I hung up.

Just like that, we'd both reverted to my childhood patterns. Not to be too psychoanalytic about it, but my problems all started at birth—really. You see, I was born with a facial deformity. The two sides of my face were asymmentrical. To fix it meant surgery. That meant money. We didn't have any.

After my father met his untimely demise, my mother moved us from Tampa to Boca—which, as I said before, has some of the world's finest plastic surgeons. And she set out to find a man who would provide the financing. So, yes, she loved me. At the same time, there was this message: You're ugly. You're abnormal. You're not acceptable. Now imagine growing up poor and deformed in the town of the rich and beautiful. Yeah, my self-esteem was below zero.

As I said before, Mom went through a few guys before she hit the jackpot with Mort. By then, I was fifteen. That's when life started to imitate reality TV. Mort picked up the tab for my surgery, and suddenly I was like a perfect case for *The Swan* or *Extreme Makeover*.

So now you know: I'm not a natural-born Babe. Of course, most Boca Babes aren't. But hey, at least I didn't cut off my Jewish nose to spite my race as Golda Meir once said.

The thing about being a Boca Babe is that it's addictive. Once I had the new face and a taste of the bucks, I wanted more. I loved the attention I got from men and the jealous glares from other women. And to be honest, I liked the new house, the pool, the tennis lessons, the fine restaurants, the parties, the pampering. I mean, what wasn't to love after years of seeing my mom and her husbands struggle with money? Seeing my mom so depressed, and then seeing her so happy when Mort and his money came into her life, and how his money helped make me acceptable—finally—to my mom. I thought that to stay happy, I had to find a rich man. Of course, this fit perfectly with Mom's plans for me.

Right now, I had to get a grip. I wasn't about to sit on my ass and analyze my mother. Or myself. I had work to do.

I called the contessa to give her a progress report.

"So here's where I am now," I summed up. "Clearly, the Indigenous People's Liberation Front is supplying Mayan rebels with arms, not food. Gladys was the group's record keeper. Now, was this of her own free will or at Miguel's behest?"

"And why did Gladys give the ledger sheet to Eulalia?" the contessa asked.

"Obviously, for safekeeping. But what—or whom—was she, and Eulalia for that matter, afraid of? Miguel? Other FLGI members? Jake Lamont, the crew boss? Does he even know about the operation?"

"Remember," the contessa said, "Gladys had recently obtained her legal status and had left the fields. Maybe her compatriots then perceived her as a threat, since she no longer had the same incentive that they did to keep quiet about the gunrunning."

"Yeah," I replied. "So one of them—or all of them—might have silenced her."

"Yes, although I hate to think of my boys and girls doing such a thing."

"But there's still something wrong with this whole

picture. The Mayan laborers were indentured servants. All their meager earnings went to pay off their slave masters—um—creditors. So where did they get the money for the weapons they were shipping back home?"

"And then there is that other sheet of paper that Gladys gave to Eulalia," the contessa said. "What could the Isis Women's Comprehensive Health and Fertility Clinic possibly have to do with any of this?"

"I have no idea. But here's one thing: that 'UD' preceding Gladys's name on the medical chart? It was probably originally 'IUD,' since the left margin was torn off. Gladys had probably gotten an intrauterine device at the Isis Clinic."

"Well, so what?" the contessa asked. "Why was she compelled to give the record of this to Eulalia? We know IUDs are fairly notorious for complications, but what could this have to do with Gladys's death by strangulation?"

"I don't know," I said, "but I'll sure as hell find out. I'm going to head out there now."

The ride into town was uneventful, aside from the usual blind Stupid User Vehicle drivers cutting me off

and a couple young self-styled studs on crotch rock-
ets—Kawasakis and such—trying to challenge me to
a drag race. Please. I outgrew the need to prove
anything to anybody the day I ended my Boca Babe
life.

I pulled up to the Isis Clinic. It was located just off
Mizner Park, the chichi little shopping plaza that is
the place to see and be seen in Boca. This wasn't
migrant farmworker territory. So what could Gladys
have been doing here?

I took off my leathers and helmet and stashed
them in my saddlebags. I proceeded to the entrance,
where discreet silver block lettering read "Isis Wom-
en's Comprehensive Health And Fertility Clinic—
We Treat You Like The Goddess You Are."

Oh-kay. I took a deep, cleansing breath, focused
on my third eye chakra, and tried to summon the
goddess within. A little yoga exercise left over from
my Boca days. However, She seemed to be on strike.
I still felt like the same mere mortal that I had
woken up as that morning.

I opened the door and entered a plush waiting
room, decorated in shades of pink and white. It was
occupied by two Boca Babes, who briefly looked up
from their copies of *Town & Country* and *Condé Nast*

Traveler to check out the newcomer. It was also occupied by a school of exotic fish in a large, built-in aquarium, but they didn't bother checking me out.

I crossed the room to a tall counter topped with a sliding frosted-glass window. The window slid open and a receptionist looked out. She was a carbon copy of the one I'd encountered at Tricia Weinstein's office the day before. I swear, sometimes I think there's a factory somewhere in Boca that stamps them out in bulk—long blond hair, fake boobs, bony butts.

The receptionist handed me a clipboard and said, "Please sign in, and give us your insurance card."

"I'm not a patient." I handed her my business card. "I'm a private investigator looking into the murder of a woman who may have been a patient here."

"I'm sorry," she said, "but I can neither confirm nor deny whether anyone has ever been a patient here. And even if she had been a patient, we couldn't tell you anything about her. We observe patient confidentiality strictly."

"Oh, that's too bad," I said. "My client, Contessa von Phul, will be most distressed to hear that."

The woman's face blanched. "I'll see if the clinic director is available," she said quickly.

"Great! Thanks so much," I replied.

In Boca, it was all about knowing what leverage to use with whom. Whereas mention of the police had worked wonders with Miguel yesterday, that would never cut the mustard on this side of town. One or two rounds on the golf course with the right people would easily rectify any little problem posed by the police. A different incentive was needed here, and the contessa was it. Like I said before, you don't mess with the contessa.

The receptionist rose and I watched her stride down a hallway. Have you ever noticed how those fake-boob women always walk as if they have broomsticks up their asses, thrusting their prized assets out there for all the world to admire? "These Tits are Made for Walkin'" seems to be their theme song.

Just as I sat down, the front door opened. I looked up to see a blast from my past—a former friend from my former life. Brigitta Larsen O'Malley was one of the reigning Babes of Boca. She was a six-foot-tall blond bombshell who had been Miss Denmark and third runner-up for Miss Universe back in the mid-eighties. Soon thereafter, she'd married now eighty-year-old Lapidus O'Malley and started her post-pageant life, which consisted of bearing Lapidus's offspring (his third set), spending his money and being Boca's most sought-after aerobics instructor. Lapidus was the senior partner in the law firm that my husband had been in, which is how our paths had crossed.

I always felt awkward whenever I ran into old friends like this. Mainly because their own awkwardness at encountering me was so evident. They wished I didn't exist. I had exposed one of the dark secrets of the Boca Babes' seemingly perfect world. Not that all of them were beaten by their husbands, but for more than a few there was that ugly truth beneath the beauty. I had broken the code of silence, and to them that made me a traitor. However, they'd deserted me when I really could have used some support, so who had betrayed whom?

But I decided to take the high road at this moment.

"Hey, Gitta," I said.

She glanced up. "Oh! Harriet!"

Her hand shot up and she nervously fingered her necklace, a thick silver link chain with a nameplate boldly stamped *Tiffany & Co*. Her bust was stamped *Versace* and her bag, *Vuitton*. God, she was a walking billboard. Why not just hang a big sign saying For Sale around her neck?

Her pale-blue eyes slid past me to the two Babes.

"Heather! Laurel!" She walked past me and a flurry of air-kissing ensued among the trio.

"Love your Jimmy Choos," Heather/Laurel said to her.

"Thank yooouuu!" Brigitta squealed. "I got them in the city when we were up there this weekend."

"Oh, we were just there, too. You know we just got a new penthouse on Park Avenue," the other Heather/Laurel said.

Brigitta sniffed, then pulled out a tissue from her bag and blew her red-tipped nose. I recognized the signs. Miss Copenhagen was now Miss Cokehead.

They continued their insipid conversation. I had become invisible. There was my former life before my eyes, displayed in its near entirety for my viewing horror. Nothing but shopping and schmoozing, schmoozing and shopping. Some might say that for me it was Shopping Paradise Lost. But I say it's Hog Heaven Gained.

In a few minutes, the door leading to the inner sanctum opened, and Miss Tits, the receptionist, announced, "Ms. Horowitz, the doctor will see you now."

She ushered me down a hallway where various

medical personnel were milling around. We passed some examination rooms, where I caught sight of those metal stirrups—you know the ones I'm talking about. Ugh! Is there any other piece of medical equipment that bears a greater resemblance to a medieval torture device? Okay, a dentist's drill, maybe. But it's close.

We entered an office, where a man was seated behind a large oak desk. He was your typical GQ Man of Style. In his forties, tall, with dark hair and that oh-so-distinguished gray at the temples matching perfectly with his slate-colored eyes. Immaculate grooming and attire. Crisp shirt cuffs with gold links extended just the right distance beneath his white lab coat. He must have been a real hot item around town. Boca Babe wannabes were always on the lookout for Dr. Right.

He smiled, displaying a nice set of porcelain veneers, and reached out a hand. "Hello, Ms. Horowitz. I'm Dr. Steve Farber, the clinic director," he said.

Framed diplomas on the wall behind him identified him as a graduate of the Albert Einstein College of Medicine, a board-certified member of the American College of Obstetricians and Gynecologists, blah, blah, blah. Okay, so I guess he wasn't a total quack. I shook his hand.

"Please have a seat," he said, and I did. Miss Tits left.

"Candi tells me that you are investigating the murder of a possible patient on behalf of the contessa. Naturally, we are eager to help in any way we can. Normally, of course, we do not release patient information, but in view of the tragic circumstances, that changes things. If indeed the victim was a patient here and we can help bring her killer to justice, it's the least we could do. Now, what is the woman's name and what makes you think she may have been one of our patients?"

"Gladys Gutierrez. I have acquired what looks like part of her medical chart. Of course, I'm not at liberty to say where I got it, as I'm sure you understand," I put in before he could ask.

"Absolutely, no problem," he said. "May I see the record?" I handed it to him. "Yes, it does look like it's from one of our charts. Let's find out." He pushed an intercom button and said, "Candi, will you please see if we have a file on a Ms. Gladys Gutierrez?"

"Yes, Doctor," a disembodied voice replied.

"Perhaps while we wait, I can tell you a little about our clinic," he offered. It was the salesman in him talking, I could tell.

"Sure," I said. You never knew what useful information could come from people running off at the mouth.

"We are proud to be one of the leading women's health and fertility clinics in the nation," he began. "We provide a comprehensive array of services for women of all ages. We offer everything from basic exams to a full range of contraceptives, prenatal care, labor and delivery and outpatient surgery. We have a complete surgical suite on site and a full operating room staff, so we're able to do almost any gynecological procedure and send the patient back to the comfort of her own home the same day. We also provide a full spectrum of gynecological reconstructive and cosmetic procedures, including vaginal retightening, hymen reconstruction and labia reduction."

"Oh, really?" I said. "Can you restring my guitar, too?"

He stopped a moment, then continued. "As I'm sure you can imagine, Ms. Horowitz, these are not laughing matters to many women. Take hymen reconstruction, for instance. As you know, here in South Florida our community is greatly enriched by having a diverse, multicultural population. But, as you may be aware, in some cultures the men will only marry virgins. So, if a young lady has had premarital relations, should that condemn her for life? We like to think not. With a hymen reconstruction, she can restore her virginity and go on to live a fulfilling life as a wife and mother. We take substantial pride in our culturally sensitive practice in this regard.

"Or, let's take labia reduction. With the proliferation of nudity in the media these days, many women feel that their genitalia just don't measure up to the ones their husbands or boyfriends are looking at in *Playboy* or on the Internet or whatnot. So with a little nip and tuck, that problem is easily corrected. And then, of course, there's vaginal retightening. Naturally, the birth canal stretches during delivery, and it doesn't spring right back, so to speak, afterward. So, many women fear that they won't be able to please their husbands in the same way as before. So again, that problem can be easily corrected.

"In essence, Ms. Horowitz, here at the Isis Clinic, we promote a woman's sense of her divine womanhood. These fairly minor surgical procedures make radical transformations in the patient's self-esteem, life satisfaction and empowerment."

Okay, I got it—pussy power. When did feminism get co-opted by the medical establishment?

"Furthermore," the good doctor went on, oblivious to my internal lament, "our greatest point of pride is our fertility program. We offer the very latest in assisted reproductive technology—all the enhancements of in vitro fertilization, including intracytoplasmic sperm injection, assisted hatching and zygote intrafallopian transfer. And of course we take a holistic approach that treats the mind, body and soul. We offer counseling, meditation and all the Eastern approaches. Our success rate is one of the highest in the country—in the world, for that matter."

"Well, it sounds like you've got a pretty good gig going here," I said amiably.

At that moment, Candi walked in with a green manila file folder under her arm. "Here is the patient chart you requested, Doctor," she said.

"Thank you, Candi." She left and he looked at me. "So, Ms. Gutierrez was indeed a patient here." He opened the file and leafed through it. "Okay, I see where the missing sheet belongs, but I can't imagine how it got out of this file. That 'UD' that's on that sheet of paper? It was originally IUD, intrauterine device."

Of course, I already knew that, ace detective that I am.

He went on, "She was fitted with an IUD here

about two years ago. She came back a month later for a follow-up, and there were no problems noted. That was her last visit. She would have been due back a year later."

"That would be about the time she was murdered. Is there anything else in there about her? At this stage of my investigation, any information—no matter how irrelevant it might seem—could turn out to be important."

He leafed through the chart some more. "Well, she didn't know her date of birth, or even the year, so we judged her to be in her early twenties. Her physical exam showed no remarkable findings. Her vital signs were all within normal ranges. She didn't complain of any problems. Basically, she was just seeking a reliable method of contraception, so we recommended the IUD. It's long-term and doesn't require any action on the part of the patient. Plus, the male partner need not be aware of its use. In some cultures, the men believe that a woman who is using contraception must be 'loose.' So, the IUD puts the woman in control of her own body, without upsetting the traditional gender roles or inciting domestic violence. So that's about it. Gladys was basically a healthy young woman. What a tragic loss of life."

"Dr. Farber," I said, "let me be blunt." As if I was ever anything but. "At the time she came here, Gladys Gutierrez was an illegal immigrant working in the tomato fields. Health insurance was not part of her 'employee benefits package.' Your clinic would appear to serve an entirely different class of clientele. How is it that Gladys came to this clinic?"

"Ms. Horowitz, with all due respect, I fear you may have misjudged us. We here at the Isis Clinic firmly believe that health care is every woman's right. We are strongly committed to providing health care access for all populations and so we do some pro bono work. We employ a part-time health educator who does outreach to the migrant farmworkers."

"Cool," I said. There didn't seem to be anything more for me to ask. "All right, thanks for your time. The contessa will be most grateful."

"I was happy to help," he said. "I only wish I had more information to give you. To tell you the truth, I'm disappointed myself. I was hoping there would be a major clue in this file, but it doesn't seem like it."

"Well, you never know what might become significant later," I said, and got up to leave.

"Ms. Horowitz, it has been a pleasure to meet you," he said. "Should you or any of your family and friends ever be in need of women's health care, I hope you'll keep us in mind." He handed me his business card. "Have you had your annual pelvic exam?" he asked.

"Um, I might be a couple years overdue," I admitted. Well, I hadn't seen any action down there in about that long, so why bother?

"Well, as I'm sure you know, prevention and early detection are the keys to good health. Take care of your body, and it will take care of you. You really should make an appointment with us."

"All right, I will," I said. As if.

I stopped by the laundromat on my way home and threw my tomato-infused clothes into the washing machine. I missed having my laundry picked up and delivered to my door. As a Boca Babe, my idea of dirty laundry was kibitzing about the neighbors.

I sat there and watched the clothes spin around and around, the water turning redder and redder. The circular motion was like a mandala, putting me into a meditative frame of mind—almost like riding my Hog, but not quite.

It was in that half trance that it suddenly struck me. Eureka! I'd found it—the secret Boca Babe factory that I'd long suspected of existing! The Isis Clinic.

Think about it. They were on the cutting edge of fertility technology. There was only one inescapable conclusion: the Isis Clinic was producing clones! Boca Babe clones, to be exact. Not that this epiphany got me any closer to finding Gladys's killer.

CHAPTER 10

I sat on the porch, drank my Hennessy, and expounded my Boca Babe Clone Theory to Lana. She opened her jaws wide, drew back her lips to expose her deadly weapons, then slowly closed her trap again. Had I just witnessed a gator yawn? Okay, I got the message. She wasn't too impressed with my theory.

Yeah, so maybe I had jumped the gun a little. On reconsideration, it may have been a little far-fetched. After all, a human clone had never been produced, notwithstanding the claims of that wacko cult a while back. Anyway, clones didn't just materialize in full adult form. If Boca was populated by Babe clones now, they would had to have been created at least twenty years ago. Not a likely possibility, I had to admit.

Just then the phone rang.

"Harriet, you will not believe—I've met the most wonderful man!"

Damn! I knew it, I knew it, I knew it. My mother

was incapable of spending a couple weeks alone without casting out the nets to see what she could catch.

"So, tell me about him," I said through gritted teeth.

"He is completely charming, thoughtful, intelligent. We spent the day on Saint Lucia together and had a marvelous time. And guess what? He lives right in Boca. Sergei says—"

"Sergei?"

"The KGB man."

"What? You're seeing a KGB man?"

"Of course not, don't be silly. I'm seeing Leonard Goldblatt. He's Sergei's counterpart in the lecture series. He's retired CIA."

Oh, well, that was different. What a relief.

Shit! My mother had hooked up with a spook. Of course he was charming and smart—that's exactly what he was trained to be! Who knew what his true nefarious plans were?

"Mom," I said with a sigh, "what do you really know about this man? He could be—"

"Harriet, I do not appreciate your tone. Why do you want to deny me a little happiness in the twilight of my life?"

Well, as you might imagine, the conversation went downhill from there.

My mother, the Drama Queen. Twilight of her life, my ass. She was in her prime. And I'd be damned if I'd let some secret agent stranger steal her heart as a prelude to stealing her money. I might not have much money, nor no longer need much of it to be happy, but my mom did. Plus, it kept her off my back.

The problem was, being a Botox Babe, Mom made an ostentatious display of her maritally acquired megabucks. Like the contessa, she dripped designer duds and diamonds. So, no doubt, this covert operative, or whatever the hell he was, was surely out to make some acquisitions of his own. I had to get the goods on this guy and expose his true intentions.

Unfortunately, that would have to wait till later. Right now, I had a killer to catch.

I woke up early, and piloted my airboat to land, all the while fretting about my mother. At the dock, I unloaded the Hog and then rode to Tricia's residence at the Trailing Vines Country Club.

After being vetted by the security guard at the community entrance gate, I proceeded to the house. Well, I suppose it was a "house" the way an ocean liner is a "boat." "Castle" would be a more apt term, I guess. It had turrets and all. The only thing missing was a moat.

A gardener was trimming the hedges out front. He stopped work to listen to my Hog as I pulled up the driveway. Can't blame him—that V-twin vibe beats the sound of hedge clippers any day.

I rang the bell and immediately there was a flurry of barking inside. I hoped I wouldn't have to fend off another Coco. I stood there, cooling my heels. I guess it would take a while for someone to get from one end of this château to the other. Just as I was about to ring again, the door was opened by a clean-cut, bespectacled man about Tricia's age. He was wearing a lime-colored golf shirt and matching plaid shorts. Chic for Boca Raton males.

A chocolate Labrador retriever was running around his feet, wagging its tail.

"Hi, Harriet Horowitz?" he (the man, not the dog) asked. "Tricia's expecting you. I'm Mark Cohen, her husband. C'mon in. She's upstairs decorating the nursery for the baby. This is Max," he said, indicating the dog.

Unlike Coco, this one was so cute that I just had to bend down and scratch its ears. I missed my former mutt, a shih tzu I'd named Diva Dog. As a Boca Babe, my dog had owned more clothes and toys than most people's children. But I had to admit that with her delicate sensibilities, she was probably better off with her new owners in their plush condo than with me in my swamp hut.

Then I remembered that I had my Dirty Harriet image to uphold, so I stood up. After all, when did you ever see Dirty Harry petting anything?

I stepped into the foyer, which was flanked on either side by built-in niches displaying opulent oil paintings illuminated from above by recessed lighting. The painted dome ceiling featured blue sky with white clouds and a few cherubim and seraphim peeking out at the edges. The Sistine Chapel look was big in Boca.

A double staircase led to the upper floor. I expected to see Scarlett O'Hara come floating down in her drapery ball gown.

We walked up, and I heard the sounds of the Eagles' "Hotel California" coming from a room down the hall. As we approached, the music grew louder. We entered the room. Tricia had her back turned to us as she half danced, half worked, hanging a framed drawing of a smiling elephant on the far wall. A stack of more pictures and a CD player, the source of the music, were on the floor. A crib stood at one end of the room underneath a hanging mobile of circus animals. Next to that was a changing table and a diaper pail. At the other end of the room was a dresser topped with a collection of teddy bears. The Good Life awaited this kid.

"Tricia," Mark called. She didn't hear him. He repeated it louder and she turned around.

"Oh, hi." She bent over and turned the music down, struggling a little to get back up, her protruding belly putting her off balance. Mark walked over to help her get upright.

She looked younger and more relaxed than she had at the office, probably because she had on less makeup, or because her clothes—flowered capris topped by a large Polo shirt—were more casual than the couture maternity suit she'd had on when I last saw her.

"I'll let you two talk," Mark said, and looked at his watch. "I've got a tee time with some clients in half an hour. Tricia, have you seen my golfing glove?"

"No, honey," she replied. "When was the last time you had it? Maybe you should retrace your steps. Or maybe it's in your golf bag."

"Yeah, I'll check," he said and headed out the door.

"Oh, honey," she called, "don't forget we're having company tonight for Mom's birthday. I'll be wearing my red-and-white Escada suit, so you should pick out something to match."

"Right," he said, and left.

She shot me a conspiratorial smile, like we were two sorority girls giggling about their boyfriends. "Mark is a little absentminded," she said indulgently. "If I wasn't around to keep his life organized, he'd fall apart."

Well, to each his own. If anybody tried telling me what to wear, he might as well sprout wings, because his ass would be flying out the door.

"Anyway," Tricia said, "do you mind if I keep working while we talk? I've got to get these pictures up this morning. I've just got so much to do before the baby comes. It's my first one, so I had to start from scratch with all the supplies and decorations and everything. The pregnancy was a wonderful surprise, but with all my work and all the preparations here, I'll admit I'm feeling a little overburdened."

"Sure," I said. "Can I do anything to help?"

"Oh, no thanks," she said, and started rolling paper up the wall again. Perfectionists. They might be overburdened to the gills, but would they ever let anyone help? Of course not. No one could do anything as well as they could themselves.

In the background, the Eagles were now singing "Witchy Woman." Coincidence or cosmic synchronicity?

"So, what did you want to ask about Gladys?" Tricia inquired, her feet moving to the beat.

"Well, was there anything unusual about her behavior in the days before her disappearance?"

"No, I wouldn't say so," Tricia said. "Of course, she was only with us a couple weeks, so I didn't know her all that well. I wouldn't really know what was usual or unusual for her. She did a good job for us, like I said. Always did all her tasks just as I instructed."

Now, that seemed a little unusual to me. Could anyone really please a perfectionist?

Tricia continued, "When she wasn't working, she pretty much stayed in her room. She did go sit out by the pool once in a while, but that's about it."

"Did she express any concerns or worries to you before she disappeared?"

"No, but of course we didn't really talk, other than about the household tasks. Her English was pretty limited. Anyway, I make it a practice not to get too friendly with people who work for me, both at work and at home. It's a bad idea, creates role confusion."

Of course. We wouldn't want any human-to-human contact across caste lines or anything.

"How about visitors?" I asked. "Did she ever have any?"

"She had a little friend that came a couple times. Eu-something. Eunice?"

"Eulalia," I said.

"Yes, that's it."

At that moment, Mark entered the room. "Tricia, have you seen my red Saint Laurent tie?" he asked. "I wanted to wear it tonight."

"No, I haven't," she replied. "Why don't you wear the Roberto Cavalli one? That'll match well."

"Yeah, okay," he said, and left.

If these two were trying to impress me with the designer name-dropping, they were wasting their time.

I resumed my questioning. "So nothing different happened in the days before Gladys's disappearance?"

"No, sorry," she said, hammering a nail into the wall. "I wish I could be more helpful. Anyway, I already told all this to the police."

"Do you think I could talk to some of the other

household staff who worked here at the same time as Gladys? They might have gotten to know her a little better than you did, so they might be able to shed some more light on things."

"Well, the police already talked to them, so I don't see what good it would do, but okay. I'll get you a list of their names and numbers. We don't have anyone live in, except the housekeeper who replaced Gladys, and of course she didn't know Gladys since she came after her. If you can hold on a minute, I'll go make the list."

She left and there I was again, stuck in a room that provided no opportunity for snooping. There was nothing in here but teddy bears and diapers.

Tricia came back with a computer-generated list. Naturally, Ms. Organized must have had all the names, addresses and phone numbers of anyone she'd ever had any contact with stored in a database. I wondered what terms you'd search under to pull out the servants from the family members, friends and clients. Riffraff? Commoners?

"Here are the names of the gardener, the cook, the dog walker and the car detailer. They all still work for us," she said.

Just then the doorbell rang. "Oh, that must be the

caterer delivering the hors d'oeuvres for tonight," she said. "And I'm expecting my personal trainer any minute. So, if there's nothing else you want to ask…."

I was being dismissed again. But that was cool. I had to get out of this place. I was getting some wicked flashbacks of my past life with its cast of thousands all there to support the lord and lady of the manor.

I said goodbye to Tricia and roared off on my Hog, letting out a deep breath of relief. Man, how much simpler my life was now. Sure, recovery hadn't been easy, but I wouldn't go back to that fairy tale if my life depended on it. There were too many monsters hiding in those woods.

CHAPTER 11

Okay, I know—where do I get off talking about monsters in the woods, when I live next door to an alligator? Well, at least I know Lana is there. It's the enemy you can't see that you've got to worry about.

Right now, I had other worries. I had to track down the truth about Leonard Goldblatt, my mother's new squeeze. I rode to my office. There, the first thing I did was look him up in the phone book. Naturally, he wasn't listed. So I got on the Web and looked up the phone number of the International Spy Museum in Washington. After pressing a gazillion numbers to get through the organization's voice mail system—was this supposed to be a metaphor for the challenges of the espionage experience or something?—I finally managed to get a live person in the personnel department.

"Hi," I said, "I'd like to get some information about Leonard Goldblatt, who is conducting a lecture series under your auspices aboard the *Merry Mermaid.*"

"One moment, please."

Before I had a chance to respond, I was put on hold. The theme music from *Goldfinger* came on the line. I drummed my cold fingers on my desk. Then the *Mission: Impossible* theme came on. This was followed by *The Spy Who Loved Me* and *The Lady Vanishes*.

Okay, that did it. Here I was trying to save my mother from the spy who would soon purport to love her and make her and her money vanish, and I was on perpetual hold.

Just then, the live person came back on.

"I have the information you asked for. According to our promotional materials, Mr. Goldblatt is a former CIA supervising special agent and one of the world's leading authorities on counterintelligence and clandestine strategies and tactics. He is on the board of directors of the Association of Former Intelligence Officers and..."

Shit! I knew I wasn't dealing with a living, breathing, sentient being. It was a robot, an android, or whatever—just reciting a canned spiel.

"I don't want the man's official freaking résumé!" I yelled into the phone. "I don't want the cover story! I want the straight scoop! The inside dope!"

There was a brief silence on the other end while the robot's tape rewound. Then it replayed, "One moment, please."

I was tortured with some more music to spy by, then a woman identifying herself as the director of human resources came on the line. I restated my wishes, just as I had learned in a class on How To Complain Effectively that I'd taken back in my doormat days: clearly state the problem, then clearly state what you would like done about it, then restate both. That trick worked about as well now as it had then—that is to say, not at all.

"I'm sorry," the woman said, "I cannot give out any information of that nature. I'm sure you realize that our employee records are confidential."

I should have known. The only way to complain effectively is the Magnum method. Unfortunately, that doesn't work with the CIA.

Now what? I knew better than to try to tackle the agency. They'd turn the tables, swoop down in the middle of the night, haul me off to some undisclosed location and interrogate me till I confessed to... something, anything.

The only other option was to run a computer background check on Goldblatt. I logged on to a national database of U.S. residents and entered his name and city. I didn't have his date of birth, but I knew he had to be at least in his sixties if he'd been a player in the Cold War. Several Leonard Goldblatts popped up, but none in that age range. I went through the full background investigation, checking public records, criminal databases and several subscription services that give P.I.s access to drivers' licenses and other information. Nothing turned up. Nada.

As far as I could determine, Leonard Goldblatt did not exist. Then again, he was CIA. He could have had his records wiped, or had used an entirely different name. Nonetheless, the fact that he left no electronic trace made me very nervous.

I decided to give it a rest for a while and let my subconscious come up with a plan.

I spent the rest of Saturday writing an interim progress report for the contessa and working a couple other cases. Then I went home to my beast buddy. We had a wild Saturday night out on the swamp, Lana snapping at turtles and whatever else happened to float by, me gazing at the night sky. As Oscar Wilde said, "We're all in the gutter, but some of us are looking at the stars."

I woke up ready to take on the world, avenge Gladys and save my mother. Unfortunately, it was Sunday, so the world wasn't ready for me. I wouldn't be able to get any interviews done on the case today, or do much about my mother, either. So I decided to mellow out with motorcycle maintenance.

I pulled the Hog up on the porch and set it on its center stand. I checked the spark plugs and replaced one. Then I checked the oil level. Having completed these tasks, I sat down for a while to bask in that virtuous feeling that comes from accomplishment.

That afternoon, I arrived at Lior Ben Yehuda's Krav Maga Center, located not far from my office on the gritty outskirts of Boca. My body still felt a little battered from the week's misadventures, and I figured the best thing for it would be to get some movement into those joints and muscles. Krav Maga hadn't yet made it to the fancy-ass athletic clubs of Boca, thank God (Goddess, whatever). That would be the end. Krav Maga is about street fighting. I couldn't quite picture it being practiced by Boca Babes, most of them aerobics fanatics who go to class wearing three bras to keep their assets frozen in place while they jump up and down. I like to practice Krav Maga the way it was meant to be, in ratty sweat clothes and scruffy old gym shoes and with a scrappy attitude.

That day Lior greeted me at the door as class was about to get started.

"*Shalom*, Harriet," he said.

"*Shalom Aleichem*, Lior," I replied. Yoga has its *namasté*; Krav Maga has its *shalom*.

Lior is an Israeli ex-commando who trained with the masters, the original students of the man who developed the method for use in the Israeli War of Independence back in 1948. He's six foot three and a lean mean fighting machine. Picture The Terminator as a Sephardic Jew.

Given his background, Lior is a little cocky. He likes to strut down the street like John Travolta in *Saturday Night Fever*. He eagerly awaits sundown each Sabbath so he can go hit the clubs on Miami's South Beach.

"When you going to go out with me, foxy lady?" Lior asked. This was his standard refrain. Lior was one of the few—okay, the only—straight men in my post-Babe life who wasn't intimidated by the Dirty Harriet thing. It was clear that strong women—physically and mentally—turned him on.

But I wasn't turned on by Lior—really! It was a

long way from my swamp abode to South Beach—
and not just geographically. So Lior went through the
ritual of asking me out just to test me. I had told him
we could go out when peace came to the Middle
East. And we both knew when that would be.

That afternoon we started class, as usual, with car-
diovascular, strength building and flexibility exercises. Then we reviewed the body's vulnerable points
to be targeted when fending off an attack—back of
the neck, temples, eyes, throat, knees, groin. After
that, we practiced defenses against a variety of
punches and kicks. We went through several repeti-
tions of each attack, the idea being to ingrain the defensive moves in the mind so that they become
second nature in an actual combat situation.

I left the class feeling like a born-again badass.
Once I had discovered the mental and emotional
benefits of Krav Maga, there was no going back. And
what I like most about the method is its fundamen-
tal rule: there are no rules. That suits my inner vigilante to a T.

I rode back home, thinking how much better my
body felt after its workout. That got me to thinking
about bodies in general—how they have tales to tell.
Maybe Gladys's body had a tale to tell, but one that

wasn't in the police summary I had read. If so, it would be in the autopsy report. I decided to visit the county coroner in the morning. My inner vigilante was rested, restored and ready to roll.

CHAPTER 12

The coroner, Dr. Hugo Hefner, graciously agreed to see me after Contessa von Phul called in a favor with him. So I hopped on the Hog and headed north on the Turnpike to the county morgue in West Palm.

The morgue was located in the basement of the public hospital. I got lost a couple times in the maze of corridors before I finally reached it. I pushed open the large swinging doors and looked around for the ubiquitous Babe wannabe receptionist. There wasn't one in sight. Guess those government budget cutbacks were taking a bite out of the medical examiner's staff.

"Hello!" I called.

Beyond another set of swinging doors I heard a clattering as something dropped to the floor, followed by an expletive. There was a shuffling and the doors were pushed open, revealing a wizened old man with a long white beard. His mass of white hair was backlit by the glow of overhead surgical lamps in the room behind him, creating a halo effect. He had on a long white lab coat that flowed almost to the floor. He was holding both hands up in front of him. His hands were covered in latex gloves, which were covered in blood.

Basically, your standard-issue mad scientist. Think Gene Wilder in *Young Frankenstein*, but about forty or fifty years older.

I guess I must have let my facade of imperturbable cool slip, because he cracked, "What'd you expect? A guy in a red silk robe sipping a martini?"

"Of course not," I said, although that was exactly the image I'd had.

I started to introduce myself. "I'm—"

"I know who you are, young lady," he crowed. "I looked you up after the contessa called, and saw that I did the postmortem on your old man after you iced him. Nice shot."

"Oh, uh, thanks," I said.

"Well, don't just stand there," he said. "C'mon back. I'm a busy man. I got stiffs to see, cadavers to cut."

Wait a minute. He expected me to go in *there?* With the *bodies?*

Yeah, okay. I was Dirty Harriet, after all. I asked myself my standard WWHD question in these situa-

tions: what would Harry do? The answer was obvious.
In I went.

The room was walled with those sickly pale-green
bricks that seem to be popular in public hospitals
and public schools. A few steel gurneys were scattered
around, each covered with a sheet from beneath
which a tagged toe peeked out. One gurney in the
center held the uncovered body of a young woman.
Her chest was cut open, but her prefab double-Ds
were on the job, standing straight up. It was a little
poignant; the Grim Reaper had come knocking, but
the knockers were still going strong.

Hefner glanced at the corpse.

"Fell overboard off the *Hedonist*," he mumbled,
naming a yacht owned by a certain notorious trust
fund baby over in Palm Beach. "Wasn't drowning that
did her in, though," he went on. "It's a little known
fact, but these saline implants can serve as flotation
devices. Remember that the next time you're on the
water. The life you save just might be your own." He
eyed my chest. "Well, maybe not," he amended. "This
one probably OD'd. I'll have to run a tox screen."

"So, about Gladys Gutierrez?" I cut in.

"Yeah, I got the autopsy file out before you came
up. C'mon into my office." He peeled off his gloves

and dropped them into a biohazardous waste container. He led me past the gurneys into a room the size of a broom closet and picked up a file from a gray metal desk.

"As you already know, she died of strangulation. Had been dead about four days. Looked as if she'd been attacked from behind and put up quite a struggle. Almost all of her nails were broken. No signs of sexual assault."

"Were there any other findings that were remarkable in any way?"

"Well, let me see." He leafed through the file.

"Five foot two…" he mumbled, "ninety-four pounds…had had a broken left wrist at one time that hadn't healed too well—it had probably never been set…teeth weren't in the best of shape—lots of cavities that had never been filled…oh, she'd had a hysterectomy at some point in her life…otherwise, looked like she'd been a healthy young woman."

I thought over what he'd just said. Something didn't make sense.

"A hysterectomy?" I asked. "I've been told that she had an IUD put in about a couple years before her death. How could she have an intrauterine device if she didn't have a uterus?"

"Well, there's no way of telling when she had the hysterectomy. It wasn't real recent, because the abdominal incision was fully healed. But at the same time, the body was fairly decomposed, so it would be impossible to pinpoint a specific time frame."

"Why would an otherwise healthy young woman get a hysterectomy?" I asked.

"Could be any number of reasons. Fibroid tumors, endometriosis, cervical lesions. It could be because of the IUD itself. They can cause some pretty severe complications, sometimes to the point where a hysterectomy becomes the only solution."

"Hmm," I said. "Anything else in the file that you can think of that might be helpful here?"

He turned a page. "Oh, yeah. There was a single red thread embedded in her neck. Silk."

"So whatever was used to strangle her had red silk in it?"

"Very likely." He set the file down and motioned for me to precede him out of the office. Back in the autopsy room, he wheeled the gurney with Miss Flotation Devices over to a vault in the wall, slid her in, slammed the steel door behind her and bolted it. It had such a final ring to it. I felt my stomach sink. The girl had set sail on the *Hedonist*, crossed the river

Styx and come ashore in Hades. It was a classic Greek tragedy.

"Well, thanks for your help, Doc," I said.

I found my way back out of the labyrinth and into the parking lot. Putting on my gear, I mounted my trusty steed and went west.

I turned south on the turnpike, then got off on Glades Road and headed for, well, the Glades.

I rumbled along the two-lane road, watching the tall white egrets stroll majestically along the canals that lined either side. Up in the distance, I saw the headlights of an approaching vehicle. The lights reflected off the blacktop, creating watery mirages on the surface.

Suddenly, the vehicle seemed to have crossed over into my lane. Damn these oblivious South Florida drivers!

There were still a few hundred yards between us, and I let off the throttle to slow down, waiting for the vehicle to drift back into the other lane. But, it wasn't drifting. I downshifted and put the brakes on. As the car came closer, I could see it was one of those omnipresent Stupid User Vehicles. Figures. Man, were these SUV drivers obnoxious.

Move over! I thought. *Moveovermoveovermoveover!*

It wasn't moving over. The headlights were bear-

THE NEXT NOVEL™

An Important Message from the Editors

Dear Reader,

Because you've chosen to read one of our fine novels, we'd like to say "thank you"! And, as a special way to say thank you, we're offering to send you two more novels similar to the one you are currently reading, and a surprise gift – absolutely FREE!

Please enjoy the free books and gift with our compliments...

Pam Powers

Peel off Seal and Place Inside...

THE EDITOR'S "THANK YOU" FREE GIFTS INCLUDE:

▶ Two NEW Harlequin® Next™ Novels

▶ An exciting surprise gift

YES! I have placed my Editor's "thank you" Free Gifts seal in the space provided at right. Please send me 2 FREE books, and my FREE Mystery Gift. I understand that I am under no obligation to purchase anything further, as explained on the back and opposite page.

PLACE
FREE GIFTS
SEAL
HERE

356 HDL EE35   156 HDL EE3T

FIRST NAME	LAST NAME

ADDRESS

APT.#   CITY

STATE/PROV.   ZIP/POSTAL CODE

Thank You!

(H-NXT-04/06)

The Reader Service — Here's How It Works:

ing down on me. My right hand and foot were squeez-
ing on the brakes with all my strength. I had no
choice—I had to run off the road. I bounced into the
stubbly grass that made up the shoulder.

The idiot was still heading straight at me. I could
now make out an outline of the driver, cell phone
pressed to ear. Damn it! I continued bouncing across
the grass, dust kicking up all around me. Oh, shit! I
was headed right into...the canal!

A startled egret flapped its wings and took off just
as I went into the water with a mighty splash.

I felt the Hog sink beneath me. I struggled to get
my helmet off and shrug out of my leather jacket. I
kicked my feet and pushed my arms down against the
water. Finally, I sputtered to the surface.

"Asshole!" I yelled at the disappearing vehicle,
and gave it the finger.

Then I started swimming toward the shore.

Suddenly, out of the corner of my eye I glimpsed
a log floating by. Wait a minute...that was no log, it
was a gator snout, and it was coming right at me!

I frantically stroked over to the bank of the canal
and pulled myself up onto land just as the fiend's jaws
opened an inch from my heels.

I lay there on the grass, gasping for breath. God,

how I hate Boca drivers! And my Hog—my baby! It was sunk. There wasn't a trace of it on the water's surface. And after I'd just done all that maintenance, too!

I sat up and put my head in my hands. The stubbly grass cut through my wet pants. I felt as if I were sitting on a porcupine.

I looked up and down the road. It was deserted. I had to get help. Sure, I'm one self-reliant motorcycle mama, but even I couldn't pull this bike out of this canal myself.

I pulled my cell out of my pocket and shook off the water. I pushed number one on my speed dial. As a Boca Babe, number one on my speed dial had been Saks. Now, it was a different kind of shop. Incredibly, the phone worked.

"Greasy Rider Bike Shop," a voice answered. It was Chuck, the shop's owner and my good buddy.

"Chuckles!" I gasped. "My ass is grass and my Hog is bogged! Come get me, pal."

CHAPTER 13

After I called Chuck, I called the cops. Not that I expected them to be of any help, but I did need them to come out and write an accident report for insurance purposes. Then I sat there on the banks of the canal for another forty-five minutes, shifting from cheek to cheek as the prickly grass cut into my butt. Several cars passed and a few stopped to ask if I needed help, but I told them it was already on the way.

Finally, a flatbed tow truck pulled up and Chuck climbed out of the driver's seat. He hooked his thumbs on to his platter-size silver belt buckle and hoisted his low-slung jeans up to his beer belly, which protruded from under a black T-shirt with cutoff sleeves. He took off his baseball cap, wiped sweat off his bald head, and stroked his goatee.

He looked like a refugee from *The Jerry Springer Show.*

"What in tarnation have you gotten yourself into

this time, Harriet?" he asked. "You look sorrier than a broke-dick dog."

"Nice to see you, too, pal," I replied. "Just haul my Hog out, will you? I'll fill you in later."

"Sure, no sweat," he said, wiping his brow again. "I brought help."

The passenger door opened and a pair of black rubber flippers emerged. They were followed by a short, trim, black rubber-suited body and finally a face covered with a diving mask. Who the hell was this, the Freeway Frogman?

The would-be Navy SEAL removed his mask and I recognized him as Enrique, Chuck's lover. That's right, Chuck is that most jarring of human contradictions—a gay redneck. Instead of a Confederate flag in the back window of his truck, he has a gay pride rainbow sticker.

Chuck had fled his native Georgia chased by a couple good ol' boys and their hound dogs, who were bound and determined to "bag a fag" that night. He crossed the state line doing ninety on his tricked-out Shovelhead, leaving his pursuers in the dust, and never looked back.

South Florida is considerably more receptive to gays than the Deep South. Yeah, I know it's confus-

ing, but politically and socially speaking, South
Florida is north of the South. Now, don't get me
wrong—we have our share of bigoted dumbasses
around here. It's just that they're so scared shitless by
the "alien invasion" of our shores that they can't be
troubled about gays. Their pea brains just aren't
capable of multitasking. So Chuck and other gays
are relatively safe, unlike poor Gladys and other immigrants.

Anyway, it was a good bet that Georgia wasn't on
Chuck's mind. But the plain fact remained: you can
take the boy out of redneck country, but you can't
take the redneck out of the boy. There he stood, in
all his guts 'n' glory.

Enrique flip-flopped over to me and kissed me on
both cheeks. "This is so exciting!" he said. "I just got
my diving certification last week. Point me to the
sunken treasure!"

Oh, great. As if I needed a dead novice fanatic
diver on my conscience. But what choice did I have?

"It went in about there," I said, pointing to the tire
tracks in the grass. "Watch it, there's a gator in there."

"Hold up, Ricky," Chuck said. "Lemme fetch my
varmint rifle."

He reached into the cab of the truck and pulled a

sawed-off shotgun down from the gun rack. "I think we just might get us some supper right here. Might get a fine pair of boots outta the deal, too."

Enrique shrugged on an oxygen tank and inserted the mouthpiece. Chuck went to the back of the truck, unhooked the tow cable, reeled it out and handed it to Enrique. "Run this through the frame under the seat, then loop it and hook it back onto itself," he instructed. Enrique nodded and waded into the water.

We watched him gradually disappear until the only sign of him was a few bubbles popping up on the surface.

Seconds passed. Then minutes. I held my breath. What was taking so long? What if he'd gotten tangled up down there? What if…?

I was painfully tracking the bubbles when suddenly something else round broke out of the water. It was a pair of glistening black eyeballs.

"Gator!" I screamed.

"Step aside, darlin'," Chuck said, and raised the shotgun to his hips. There was a *kaboom* and a spurt of water shot up six feet into the air. The gator thrashed its tail and took off in the opposite direction.

We stood there as more seconds and minutes passed. Chuck looked cool, calm and collected, but I was freaking just a little. By the time Enrique surfaced, I had picked out what to wear to his funeral and what to say to his grief-stricken mama from Panama.

He flashed us a thumbs-up, swam to the bank, pulled himself out and took off his face mask.

"That was awesome!" he exclaimed, brushing his long, dark, wet bangs out of his eyes.

Chuck rushed over and picked Enrique up in a bear hug, shotgun pointing heavenward as if to thank God for his safe return. Chuck's cool demeanor disintegrated and he wiped a tear from his eye. Well, what do you know. Guess he'd had the casket, flowers and music all picked out while putting on the nonchalant act.

"I thought I'd lost you, man," he said. "Don't know what I'd do without you."

Enrique beamed at me. Aw, shucks, love really can be sweet.

Chuck set Enrique down, walked over to the truck and flipped the switch to get the winch going. There was a groaning noise as the crank turned.

Then my baby came out of the water, looking like

the Chopper from the Black Lagoon—covered with algae and oozing mud.

I must have looked pretty pathetic because Chuck came over and put his arm around me. "Hey, cheer up," he said, pulling me into his massive chest. "I'll have you back on the road in no time. Probably just needs to dry out overnight. We'll leave it in the shop, then take a look in the morning. Hey, why don't you stay with us tonight? No sense sittin' on your duff an' mopin'."

"Oh, yeah? What's for dinner? Roadkill remoulade? Armadillo almandine? Really, no thanks, Chuckles. If you guys would just give me a ride to my boat, I'd rather be alone tonight." Like I wouldn't any other night?

"Sure," Chuck said. "Suit yourself, Lone Ranger. We love ya, anyway."

The cops finally arrived and took my report. Then Chuck positioned my Hog onto the flatbed and tied it down. The three of us climbed into the cab. I sat between the happy couple as we rode off into the sunset.

"Say, you going to the national dicks' convention in Orlando next weekend?" Enrique asked me. This wasn't a reference to a gay porn gathering. Enrique was the hotel dick, I mean, chief of security, at the

Boca Beach Hilton, and he loved to go to trade shows, where he could play with the latest high-tech surveillance devices and dish the dirt on who was doing whom in the industry.

"Nah, you know I'm not into gadgets and gossip," I said.

"Oh, come on. Come up with me. You need to get out more, meet people. How are you ever going to get laid otherwise?"

Jeez. Happy couples—they're always trying to inflict their brand of bliss on their single friends.

I'd originally met Chuck when I first got my Hog. I spent time hanging around his shop, picking up bits and pieces of maintenance know-how along the way. I still depend on Chuck for the major overhauls, but now I handle the regular upkeep myself.

Enrique had entered Chuck's life shortly after I did. Personally, I would never have pegged them as a compatible couple. But their gay matchmaker had obviously known otherwise. Go figure. Now, they've basically become my post-Babe social circle, loner that I am.

"I'm not looking to get laid," I told Enrique. After all, I had my Hog. It was always up for a ride, the pushrods pumped hard and the tires never deflated.

"Seriously, I can't go to Orlando. I've got too much work to do," I said. "Have fun."

"Okay, but trust me. When you're on your deathbed you won't be saying you wished you'd spent more of your life working. So, what are you working on these days?"

I filled them in on the Gladys case.

"You know, darlin'," Chuck said, "did it occur to you that maybe your little afternoon dip here weren't no accident? Maybe you're on to somethin' and someone's out to get your ass."

Oh. Well, no, that hadn't occurred to me. Okay, just call me Ditzy Harriet.

"Yeah, I guess you could be right," I said. "I didn't get a good look at the driver. But who could it be? If I've stumbled on to some major clue, damned if I know what it is."

"Don't know, darlin'. But you'd better watch your back."

Sounded like good advice to me. We rode on in silence till we reached the swamp.

"Thanks a lot, guys," I said, getting out of the truck. "I owe you."

"No problem," Chuck said. "Call you in the morning."

"It's been my pleasure," Enrique said. "Next time you're up shit creek without a paddle, who you gonna call? Ha! See you later, alligator!"

I piloted the airboat out to my cabin. I docked, walked in, poured myself some Hennessy and took my seat on the porch. I felt pretty bruised and battered, down and out.

Lana floated into sight off to the side of the cabin.

"Hey," I said. "I had a run-in with your cousin today. Tell the family to back off, will ya? What did I ever do to you guys?"

She didn't bat an eyelid. Of course, they never do. It's a reptilian thing.

I took a swallow of the cognac and felt it light a fire down my throat. I pulled in a deep breath and reflected on the day's events, starting with that morning's visit with the coroner.

"So Gladys had a hysterectomy," I told Lana. "And it must have been sometime in the year before her death, after she got her IUD. Because if it was before that, why would Farber have told me she had an IUD? So where did she get the hysterectomy? Not at the Isis Clinic, since Farber said she hadn't been there in a year. I'll have to ask Lupe where else she might have gotten health care."

Lana cast me a disapproving glance.

"Yeah, I know—what's this got to do with her murder, anyway? No connection, as far as I can see. And who the hell ran me off the road if it wasn't an accident? It couldn't be because of anything I found out this morning at the coroner's. How could anyone get to me that fast?

"Maybe Gladys was killed by some of those xeno-phobic bigot wing nuts who are out to rid Florida of foreigners and don't want me on their case. But how would they be on to me? I haven't come across anybody like that in my investigation. Except Jake Lamont, the crew boss, maybe. So, I'm back to the gunrunning angle. That seems more promising. Probably Gladys knew too much and had to be shut up."

Well, that brought me right back to where I'd been a couple days ago. And what about Eulalia's plea for me to personally help her, and "us"? Whom was she referring to? Damn—I wasn't making a hell of a lot of headway on the case. And I was getting a hell of a headache, besides.

"I'm gonna sleep on it," I told Lana. "Maybe I'll be like that DNA dude who went to bed, dreamed of entwined snakes, and woke up knowing that the

DNA structure was a double helix. Except I'll wake up knowing the identity of the killer!"

Lana rolled her eyes. Her meaning was clear: "In your dreams, sucka."

CHAPTER 14

I tossed and turned most of the night, the facts of the case going around and around in my mind. I finally fell asleep only to dream about—of all people—Lior, my hard-body Krav Maga instructor. Specifically, it was his hard body I dreamed of. More specifically, his hard body next to mine, his legs intertwined with mine, his fingers intertwined with mine, his tongue intertwined with—

I woke up in a hot sweat. Man, what was up with that? Like I've said before, I was not attracted to Lior. Was not, was not, was not! On the other hand, this dream sure beat the nightmares I'd had a few days ago.

My inner debate was unceremoniously interrupted by the phone ringing.

It was Chuck. "I reckon you're ready to roll," he said. "Bike dried out just fine. I replaced your spark plugs and checked all your electrical wiring. It started right up and purrs like a pussycat. Tell you what.

Things are kinda slow around here this morning. What say I come meet you in about an hour?"

"Cool," I said. "You're the man."

I took a quick shower, got dressed, made some coffee and took it with me out onto the boat.

I met Chuck at the dock, and he unloaded my Hog from the tow truck. He headed back to the Greasy Rider, and I headed to ScamBusters—two working stiffs off for another hard day at the salt mines.

My restless night had convinced me that I was only going in circles with my current line of investigation. I needed to go in a fresh direction.

I decided to find out what else had been going down in town around the time of Gladys's murder. Maybe I could find some connection among events that might give me a lead. Yeah, I know it was a long shot, but I was going nowhere fast on the track I was on, so why not?

I got to the office and turned on my computer. I logged on to the Internet and accessed the archives of the *Palm Beach Post*. I decided to skim the news from a month before to a month after Gladys's death.

Amid the usual scams and scandals, the first item of interest was that a rebel insurgency had occurred in Guatemala about three weeks before Gladys's death. After quelling the uprising, the Guatemalan government had uncovered a cache of U.S.-manufactured weapons stored in the baggage compartment of a tour bus that shuttled American tourists from their luxury hotels to the ancient Mayan ruins.

The paper had several follow-up articles to the story in subsequent days. I learned that Guatemalan officials were appealing to the U.S. government for help in finding and extraditing presumed arms smugglers operating within U.S. borders.

Okay. So right around the time of Gladys's murder, the heat was on to crack down on arms smuggling. This strengthened my theory about Gladys being killed by the Indigenous People's Liberation Front. If the feds were closing in, Gladys, the recently legalized member of the group, would have been seen as their weakest link. Okay, so I had a strong theory, but how was I going to prove it?

Deciding I needed to keep an open mind to all possibilities, I kept skimming the paper. Well, here was something else of interest. A few days before Gladys disappeared, a truck loaded with Mayan field laborers had crashed in dense early-morning fog out on Highway 441. The American driver, who had been wearing his seat belt, survived, but the sixteen Mayan workers who had been standing in the bed of the truck were all killed.

The usual band of county, state and federal politicians trotted out to express their horror at the tragedy, extend their sympathies to the families of the deceased and blame Mother Nature. A group of protesters led by Lupe demonstrated in downtown West Palm, demanding reparations for the dead workers' families and safe working conditions for all tomato pickers in the future.

Big Tomato sent out its public relations spin doctors to disavow any responsibility for the tragedy, saying the laborers' transportation was provided by contractors, so if Mother Nature wasn't at fault, the middlemen were. This flurry of activity went on for a few days, but the newspaper and the public soon lost interest since the story didn't involve either their tax dollars or their elected representatives' sex lives.

So here was another possibility. Had Gladys known something about this accident? Was there more to this story than there appeared to be? Was Big Tomato engaged in some kind of cover-up of its liability in this disastrous loss of human life? Was Gladys about to expose the truth? It wouldn't be the first time Corporate America had knocked off an informant, would it?

I had to admit, however, that this theory wasn't as strong as the gunrunning one. It was speculation, mostly.

I kept on surfing through the *Post*'s archived Web pages. Having decided to take this approach, I felt compelled to do it thoroughly, taking at least a cursory glance at every single news item, be it sports, obits or whatever.

I clicked on the society page for the week before Gladys's death. There were the usual articles about fund-raising events for this and that cause—enslaved Mayan laborers not being among them—accompanied by photos of the affluent so valiantly helping the afflicted by wearing ball gowns and sipping champagne.

One of the photos was of Tricia Weinstein and Mark Cohen. It had been taken at the Boca Heart Association benefit on Valentine's Day, the night before Gladys's disappearance. They were standing in front of some kind of huge red heart decoration, and they were perfectly matched—Tricia in a black satin gown with red trim, Mark in a black suit with red tie. I remembered how Tricia had insisted Mark match his outfit to hers that day I had been at their house. Jeez, what a way to live—always having to blend yourself into somebody's perfect picture. Oh, yeah, I guess I do know something about that kind of life.

Mark didn't appear to be bothered in the photo, though. He had on a big smile and had one arm around Tricia, his suit coat hanging open to reveal his fit torso. I noticed a speck on the end of his tie. Determined to find some imperfection in this picture-perfect duo, I clicked to zoom in on the image. Maybe his tie had dipped into the cheese dip or something. On the other hand, I guess cheese dip was too plebeian for an event like this. Oh, for God's sake, what was I babbling on to myself about? Get a grip.

But now I was obsessed and had to see what it was. I kept enlarging the photo till the speck was clearly visible. It was just some letters embroidered onto the tie: YSL, the designer logo of Yves Saint Laurent. Big deal. But wait a minute. Hadn't I heard something about a red Yves Saint Laurent tie before? That's right. When I'd been at Mark and Tricia's house, he'd asked if she'd seen that tie.

So, he had the tie on the night before Gladys's disappearance, and now it was missing. And wait another minute. Hadn't the coroner said there was a red silk thread embedded in Gladys's neck? Wouldn't a tie make a great strangulation device? Was this a little too coincidental or what?

It was time for me to have a little heart-to-heart with Mark Cohen about the night of the Boca Heart Association ball.

CHAPTER 15

The police file on Gladys indicated that Mark was employed at Cohen & Cohen Financial Planners in downtown Boca. I decided a surprise visit would be the optimal strategy so that he wouldn't have time to develop some elaborate explanation about his missing tie.

So, after a lunch of bagels and lox from Saul's Deli down the street, I rode over to Mark's office. It was located a few blocks from the beach in a medium-rise office building. Boca doesn't do high-rise; it's part of the aesthetic code. I rode the elevator to the third floor and proceeded to Suite 315.

I won't bother describing the receptionist, since you already know what's up with that. She buzzed Mark on the speaker phone.

"A Ms. Harriet Horowitz is here to see you."

"Who?"

"It's about Gladys Gutierrez," I said. She relayed the message.

"Who?" he asked again. Yeah, I guess he was as absentminded as Tricia had said.

"His former housekeeper," I told the receptionist, and she again relayed the information.

"Oh," he said. "Okay, send her in, please." Apparently, he wasn't nearly as busy as his wife.

The receptionist showed me into a private office that opened off the entry area. Mark rose to greet me from behind his desk. Today he had on a light gray suit, a matching fleur-de-lis tie and a smile.

"Nice to see you again, Ms. Horowitz," he said, shaking my hand. "But I'm a little surprised. What can I do for you?"

"I just wanted to follow up on something regarding Gladys's murder," I said.

"Sure, but if Tricia couldn't help you, I don't know how I can," he said.

"Well, I think this may have more to do with you. Would you mind telling me about your relationship with Gladys?"

"What relationship? I didn't have anything to do with her. Tricia takes care of all the household matters."

Okay, the subtle lead-in wasn't getting me anywhere. He could just keep up the denial all day. I decided to go for the full-frontal assault.

"When I was at your house a few days ago," I said, "you happened to mention a missing red tie. Guess what? Today I ran across this on the Web." I handed him the photo that I'd printed on my supercool, recently acquired laser color printer.

He looked at the picture and frowned. "So? Yeah, that's the tie, but what's the tie-in to Gladys, pardon my pun?"

"This photo was taken the night before Gladys disappeared," I said.

"I still don't get your point."

"Do you recall that night?"

"Not really. Wait, was that Valentine's Day?"

I nodded.

"Yeah, some kind of fund-raiser, right?"

"Uh-huh."

"I'm sorry, Ms. Horowitz. We go to so many of those things. They all run together after a while. Nothing stands out about that night from any other."

"So you don't remember what might have happened to your tie?"

"My tie? No, I don't know what you're getting at."

Not too swift, was he? Guess he was missing a chip or two in his central processing unit.

"Wait a minute!" Some circuits finally seemed to have connected. "Are you implying that I strangled Gladys with my tie? You can't be serious." He stared at me incredulously.

I didn't say anything, waiting for him to hang himself with his own rope, so to speak. He kept looking at me for several seconds. Then a smug smile broke out on his face.

"Oh, I get it," he said proudly, like he'd just solved some mind-bending puzzle. "You think I was banging Gladys, and she threatened to tell my wife, so I killed her. Yeah, I can see how you might think that. Here I am, a regular nice guy, not the sharpest knife in the drawer—I'm well aware of that—with a ballbusting wife who obviously runs the show. Your typical hen-pecked husband. I must be getting some on the side, right?

"Well, you couldn't be more wrong, lady. Let me tell you something—my wife is the most intelligent, most organized, most together person I know. And that's exactly how I like it. Why should I feel threatened by her success? I have absolutely no problem with it. Whatever I can do to help her with her goals, you'd better believe I'll do it. As far as I'm concerned, two hotshots in one marriage is just a setup for failure, and I'm happy to take the back seat."

Well, how about that—a post-Neanderthal husband. A pretty rare sighting, in my experience.

He continued, "Not only that, but my wife is the sexiest woman on the planet. Our love life is fantastic. So I'm sorry to disappoint you, but the Cohen-Weinstein marriage is doing just great. And it only gets better with time."

"That's great," I said.

"Now that you've reminded me about that night, I remember it well. When we got home from that party, Tricia had a surprise for me. In honor of Valentine's Day, she'd gotten a heart-shaped bikini wax at Marushka's."

He was referring to Marushka's Day Spa, a renowned Boca establishment whose eponymous proprietress was known to the cognoscenti as the "Edwardina Scissorhands" of the bikini area.

"So," Mark went on, "as you can imagine, we had some pretty hot action going that night."

Please. I'd rather not imagine. Who did this guy think he was kidding? Everyone knows one of life's basic truisms: the more someone talks about his sex life, the less of it he actually has.

"Well, thanks for setting me straight on that," I said with as straight a face as I could muster. "So you have no idea what happened to that tie?"

"As a matter of fact, since you've reminded me of that night," he repeated, "now I remember exactly what happened. At our little private après-party party, I spilled some red wine on it. A merlot, I believe. I didn't notice till the next morning, and of course by then it was ruined. So I had to toss it."

"All right," I said. "I appreciate your help." I rose to go.

"Yeah, like I said, sorry to disappoint you," he said. "But I wish you luck on the case. Even though I didn't really know Gladys too well, of course, as a human being it bothers me that this heinous crime has gone unsolved."

He walked me to the door.

"By the way," he said, "if you or any of your family or friends ever need investment advice, give me a call." He handed me his card.

Oh, here we go yet again. Was everybody in Boca on the make? Yeah, I know, stupid question.

"Sure, I'll do that," I said. As if.

When I got back to the office, I called the contessa and filled her in.

"I have to admit," I said, "that Mark was probably telling the truth. If he really had strangled Gladys with that tie, why would he be asking Tricia about it, in front of me, a year later?"

"Yes," she agreed, "it seems like this red tie had turned into a red herring."

"So, it looks like I'm back to square one. But there is an avenue of investigation that I haven't followed up yet—talking to the other members of Tricia and Mark's household staff who worked there at the same time as Gladys."

"Very well, proceed," the contessa said, and hung up.

I got out the list of names and numbers that Tricia had given me. I was able to get hold of Crystal Collins, the cook, and Jean Petit-Jean, the gardener. I have to admit that cell phones have made the P.I.'s job a little easier. Everybody has them, even the poorest of the poor, so you can pretty much get hold of anybody, anytime. I just wish the asshole drivers would hang the hell up while on the road and the yakkers wouldn't announce their business to everyone within a half-mile radius. I really don't want to hear about some old geezer's prostate problems while waiting in the checkout line at Publix.

Anyway, as it so happened, both Crystal and Jean said they would be at Tricia and Mark's in the morning, and suggested I come by to see them there. I called Tricia to get her okay, figuring she might object to my interviewing her employees while they were on her time, but she said she was fine with it.

With everything that had been happening on the case, I hadn't had a chance to check on my mother. I decided I'd better call to see if she'd eloped with Austin Powers, Sr. yet.

I dialed her cell-phone number. She picked up on the third ring.

"Hi Mom," I said. "How are things going?"

"Harriet, I'm so glad you called. I have some exciting news!"

CHAPTER 16

I braced myself. This couldn't be good.

"That's great!" I said. "What is it?"

"Leonard is hinting that he has a big question to ask me on the last day of the cruise!"

I felt a wave of nausea. This sinister stranger who seemed to have no official existence was about to ask my mother to marry him. And from the sound of it, she was about to accept. I had to give her the lowdown on this lowlife.

"Mom," I said, "I think you should know that I did a background check on him, and there's no background. I smell a rat. This whole deal is suspect. I really think you shouldn't jump into anything. Give me some time till I can find out more—"

"You did what? How dare you? I'll have you know, I am a grown woman perfectly capable of making my own decisions. I do not need you going behind my back—"

"Mom, I was only looking out for you. I—"

But the line went dead. My own mother had hung up on me. That was supposed to be my move! She had hijacked my hijinks.

I had to save her from herself. One way or another, I had to ward off her wedding to this wormy Cold Warrior. I just didn't know how yet.

At eight the next morning, I was on Tricia and Mark's doorstep. Tricia answered my ring with Max, the dog, lapping at her heels. She was dressed for work and a little out of breath.

"Hi, come in," she said. "I'm just on my way out to the office."

I stepped inside. The sound of ABBA's "Dancing Queen" blared from hidden speakers. Tricia's feet moved to the beat as she picked up her briefcase and checked her appearance in a hallway mirror.

She grinned at me. "ABBA really gets me going in the morning."

She picked up a remote, pushed a button, and the music stopped. "Okay, I'm off," she said. "Go ahead into the kitchen. Crystal is there."

I did as instructed, Max following closely behind me. I found a woman at the kitchen counter, trans-ferring some kind of stew from a large pot into Tupperware containers. She appeared to be in her late forties, with the lean, sinewy look of the long-distance running, yoga or Pilates devotee/granola freak.

"Hi, I'm Harriet Horowitz," I said. "I spoke with you yesterday on the phone."

"Yes, nice to meet you. I'm Crystal. You wanted to talk about Gladys?"

"Yes," I said. "How well did you know her?"

"Not well. I come in twice a week to prepare and refrigerate meals. Gladys had only worked here a couple weeks before she disappeared, so I saw her maybe four or five times."

"Did she ever express any concerns to you about anything? Any worries?"

"No. Of course, we didn't talk much, because her English wasn't too great."

"Was there anything unusual about her behavior? Anything that changed from when she first came till she disappeared?"

"No. Although, I did notice a couple times that she looked like she wasn't feeling well. I'm into holistic health and I just notice these things, like, her aura wasn't looking too good. So I asked her about it, and she said she felt really hot and she'd been up all night sweating. But it wasn't hot in the house. She seemed kind of out of it, too. I asked her where she'd put some pans that weren't in their usual place, and she said she couldn't remember. Well, lack of sleep will do that to you. Did you know that our society, in general, is very sleep-deprived? It's the cause of a lot of aggression, irritability, accidents. We'd all be better off as a nation if we just got enough sleep."

I wished she'd stuff the lecture.

"Anyway," she went on, "the next time I saw her, she seemed fine, so I guess it was just a virus or something."

"So you're not aware of anything unusual going on in the days before her disappearance?"

"No, that's all I know. Sorry."

"Do you remember anything about the day she disappeared?"

"No, I wasn't here that day."

"Okay, thanks a lot." I turned to leave.

"Listen," she said. "I hope you won't take offense, but your aura is a little murky. I think your system could do with some nutritional detoxification. If you like, I can set you up on a four-week trial program. It's my own custom creation—the All-Inclusive A-Z Diet Plan. It's a combination of Atkins and The Zone. I prepare and deliver all your meals twice a week. Believe me, you'll feel like a new woman. You'll have energy out the yin-yang. I have client testimonials. Take a look, it's all described in here." She handed me a brochure.

"Uh, I don't think you deliver out to my area," I said, handing it back. "Thanks anyway." On second thought, maybe Lana could use some fresh meat. Would Boca really notice one less self-promoting personal services provider?

I headed to the door to go out to talk to the gardener. As I passed through the great room, I saw a woman picking up a pair of socks off the floor. I figured it must be the housekeeper who had replaced Gladys. Adriana, Tricia had said her name was.

She glanced up with a look of disgust as she took a shirt off the back of an armchair. "Mr. Cohen such slob," she muttered. "Such rich man, such pig."

"Hi," I said, "can I bother you for a minute?"

"Yes?" she asked, nodding.

I introduced myself and explained I was seeking information about Gladys.

"No speak English too good," she said.

She seemed to have picked up *slob* and *pig* well enough. Well, why not? After all, boss-bashing is the universal pastime of the downtrodden, so I guess that would be among the first terminology that a newcomer would acquire.

I tried to communicate with her as best I could.

"Did you know Gladys?" I asked.

"No much," she said. "I know Gladys a little from Rescue Mission. We no talk much. I come here after Gladys die."

"Do you know if Gladys was worried about anything?"

She gave me a blank look. "No understand."

I couldn't think of a way to rephrase it. I decided to try a different question.

"Do you know anyone who might have wanted to harm Gladys?"

I got the blank look and the "no understand" again.

Okay, there were a couple possibilities here. Either she really didn't understand or she was pretending not to. In any case, it looked as if we were done. She probably didn't know anything that could help me, anyway, since she hadn't known Gladys much. If I decided later on that I needed to talk to her again, I'd come back with Lupe.

"Thanks," I told her, and walked to the door. Just as I reached for the handle, it swung open, nearly hitting me in the face.

"Oh, I'm sorry!" a perky voice said. It was a young woman with a long blond ponytail, a freshly scrubbed face and walking shorts. Max came bounding up and jumped on her, licking her face and wagging his tail.

"Hi, Max!" she said. "You ready for your walk, big boy?"

He wagged his tail more furiously to the point where I thought it would fall off. He seemed to like her better than his owners. Can't say I blamed him.

She looked up at me. "Hi, I'm Astrid," she said. My finely honed detective skills led me to conclude that she was the dog walker.

I decided to take the opportunity to ask some pertinent questions. I went through the spiel: who I was, what I was doing, would she mind talking to me for a couple minutes, had she known Gladys, etc. I got pretty much the same responses as I had from the others: she hadn't known Gladys much, hadn't really talked with her, Gladys had not expressed any concerns nor was she behaving unusually.

"Do you remember anything about the day she disappeared?" I asked.

"Not really. I do remember that I came in a little early that day. I had a lot of dogs to walk because another girl had called in sick. Max is in my first

walking group of the day. When I got here, Tricia
hadn't left for work yet. Anyway, Max and I went for
our walk, and when we got back, Tricia said her
housekeeper was gone. She seemed pretty pissed.
Anyway, I had to go since I had so many dogs that
day. Then a few days later, I heard Gladys had been
found dead. I was kind of freaked out."

Max was running around in circles and jumping
up and down.

"I'd better take him out," she said, taking a dog
leash off a hook near the door.

"Okay, thanks for your time," I said and followed
her and Max out.

I found Jean, the gardener, digging up some flow-
erbeds by the circular driveway. He was a Haitian
man in his fifties, with a weather-beaten face and
hands. I went through the same questions and got the
same answers. All the while he mumbled about
Tricia's overbearing supervision, how she had all his
tasks scheduled down to the hour and how everything must go according to her exact plans.

I thanked him and took off.

Okay, so Tricia was a domineering perfectionist,
Mark was an inconsiderate slob, they paid a New Age
Looney Tunes to detoxify their auras, their employees

were disgruntled and their dog was disloyal. I had
learned a lot about the Cohen-Weinstein household.
But I still hadn't learned who had killed Gladys and
why.

CHAPTER 17

Crystal's mention of Gladys's health problems reminded me that I had wanted to ask Lupe about where Gladys might have gotten her hysterectomy, since it apparently wasn't at the Isis Clinic. So I decided to stop by the Rescue Mission on my way to the office and see if Lupe was in.

I found her in her incense-filled office. She heartily welcomed me.

"Are you recovered from our adventure in the fields the other night?" she asked.

"That's old news," I said. "I've had another adventure since then." I told her about my unscheduled swim in the canal and updated her on everything I'd found out about the case since I'd last seen her, up through that morning.

"So according to Crystal, Gladys had some health problems not long before her disappearance—feeling hot, sweating, trouble remembering things."

"Sounds familiar," Lupe said. I thought I detected an edge of sarcasm.

"What do you mean?" I asked.

"Just wait about ten or fifteen years, it'll be real familiar to you, too." She looked amused. On the other hand, I must have looked puzzled.

"Hellooo?" she said. "The Big M? Menopause?"

"But Gladys was only in her twenties. How could she be having menopausal symptoms?"

"You said she'd had a hysterectomy, right? That'll cause the same symptoms. You know, the estrogen level drops and the problems start."

"Hmm," I said. "So where do you think Gladys might have gotten the hysterectomy? And if she had posthysterectomy problems, where would she go for help?"

"Beats me," Lupe said.

"Well, where would any of the Mayans go for health care?"

"They're entitled to basic preventive and emergency care, even though they're illegal immigrants. Technically, they could go to the county public health clinic. In fact, the public health workers sometimes come out to the fields to inform the workers about the clinic and their health care rights."

"Okay, wait a minute. You said 'technically' they could go there?"

"Yeah. In reality, they never go."

"Why not?"

A sly grin came across her face. "You've got to see for yourself."

She glanced out the window.

"Hey," she said. "It's a beautiful day. How about we take a ride up to the clinic so you can see? We could grab some lunch on the way back."

"Sounds good," I said.

Lupe wrapped up some work and we went outside. I always carry an extra helmet for possible passengers in my saddlebags, and I had Lupe put it on. I got on the bike, then Lupe hiked her floor-length skirt up to her knees and climbed on behind me.

I started the bike, revved up the throttle with my right hand and let out the clutch with my left. We were off, playing out our own little *Thelma & Louise* scenario.

We must have looked a little bizarre flying up the road, me in my black leathers, Lupe in her flowing red skirt, embroidered peasant top and ostentatious jewelry. Yeah, we garnered a few looks along the way. At least one bozo yelled, "Yo, dykes on a bike!" Jeez, what is it with people? Anytime two women travel together, the world assumes they're lesbians. As if the only right way for women to travel is with a male chaperone?

Anyway, Lupe had been right. It was a gorgeous day. Of course, almost all of them are here. We took our time getting up to West Palm, enjoying the blue sky, the shimmering lakes and the swaying palms along the way.

Eventually, we pulled up to the public health clinic. It was a storefront operation, located in a run-down part of town near the railroad tracks. The building boasted chipping paint and large, grate-covered windows. Behind the grates, the windows were filled with posters touting all kinds of public health messages: Get Your Kids Immunized, Get Tested for HIV.

I turned off the bike and was about to ask Lupe what the problem was when I saw it. Looming right next door was a big building sporting a bold sign saying "U.S. Immigration and Customs Enforcement."

My jaw dropped.

Lupe burst out laughing. "That's why they don't come for health care. If you were illegal, would you go anywhere near Immigration?"

I couldn't believe it. On the one hand, the government was shelling out the bucks to send public health workers out to the fields to encourage people to come in for immunization, HIV testing, etc. And on the other hand, Immigration was right there to deter all comers. What a waste of public resources!

Then again, maybe it wasn't bungling incompetence at all. Intentional subversion was more like it.

Furious, I pushed the starter and roared off, Lupe chuckling to herself behind me.

We rode a few blocks to the Intracoastal and pulled up to a waterfront restaurant. We went in and were seated outside on the patio, where we watched the boats float by. I started to chill out a little as we sat there, munching on crab legs and soaking up the beauty of the Sunshine State.

We talked about our lives, our experiences. I told Lupe about my mother's misbehavior.

"She's driving me nuts!" I said. "She won't listen to a word I say. She's about to make a major mistake, and I've got to stop her."

"You know," Lupe said, "maybe it'd be best if you just stayed out of it. How else is she going to learn from her mistakes? For that matter, maybe this guy Leonard is on the up-and-up. You really don't know that he's trying to con her."

"No, I don't believe it. I can't let this bum break my mother's heart. And anyway, I have my reputation to think about. I'm a ScamBuster. If I let my own mother get scammed, I'll be the laughingstock of Boca!"

"Look, can I share some *bruja* basics with you?"

"Some what?"

"Witchcraft wisdom. Oh, haven't I mentioned that I'm a practicing *bruja*—a Mexican witch?"

"Uh, no."

"Oh, well, don't worry. I'm not going to put a curse on you and fly off on a broom."

"Right. Okay. Sure. What would you like to share?"

"Just this: We are all responsible for ourselves. Trying to control others is a fruitless pursuit."

"That's it? That's witchcraft wisdom? I thought witches were all about controlling people with spells and all that."

"Nope. We're all about self-awareness, celebrating womanhood, connecting with nature. We do use herbal remedies, but that's about the extent of our magic. And we don't put evil out there, because we know what goes around comes around."

"So how does a Catholic schoolgirl like you become a witch?" I asked.

"Well, I originally wanted to be a nun," she said. "But I could never wrap my mind around the idea that I would always be subordinate to a priest, not to mention some other things. Then when I was in Mexico doing my fieldwork, I met some *brujas* and *curanderas*—those are healers—and their philosophy really resonated with me, so eventually I became one myself."

"So do you get together in a coven and dance around a bonfire?"

She smiled again and arched her unibrow.

"As you can see, I prefer showing to telling. So maybe you can come with me to a gathering sometime."

"Right. Okay. Sure." It all sounded pretty woo-woo to me. On the other hand, I had really developed a liking for Lupe. So who knew?

"Now that you know my life story, how about telling me a little of yours?" she asked. "How'd you become a private eye?"

I recounted how I'd unencumbered myself of a husband and an income, which were one and the same for me.

"Do you ever miss your old life?" Lupe asked.

"Sure," I said. "But all that money just costs too much."

We ate and talked some more. Hmm…this was starting to feel like a friendship.

As we were getting ready to go, Lupe said, "We're having a beach party for our clients on Saturday. It's a rare opportunity for them to relax and enjoy themselves. Why don't you join us?"

"Oh, thanks," I said, "but I'm not much of a group socializer."

"Then this is perfect for you. They don't speak much English and you don't speak any Mayan languages, so there's really no problem, is there?"

Well, when she put it like that, what could I say? Anyway, maybe it would give me a chance to try to interview Gladys's women friends again, with Lupe's help. So I agreed to go, and we headed back to Boca.

As we rode back, I got to thinking about the beach party, which got me to thinking about wearing a swimsuit. I realized I was way overdue for a bikini wax. There was no way I could show myself in public in all my hirsute glory. Much as I dreaded the prospect, a visit to Marushka's was a necessary evil.

I know, some habits die hard, but there was just no skirting the issue. I had to get my bush whacked.

CHAPTER 18

I was able to get an appointment at Marushka's for the next morning. I sat in the waiting room listening to spa music—you know, the harp, the flute and the running brook, all together on one track. I guess this was supposed to put me in a state of bliss and make me forget that I was about to have my hair pulled out by its roots. Not likely.

Eventually, Marushka emerged from behind a bead curtain, accompanied by a whiff of incense. She was a tiny, bent woman with a face wrinkled like a prune. Her head was wrapped in a magenta paisley scarf and large gold hoops hung from her ears.

"Harrrriet! Please come beck," she commanded in her Slavic accent, thick with rolling *R*'s and clipped vowels. I rose and followed her through the hanging beads. I wasn't sure if I was getting a bikini wax or a palm reading. Could I get both for the price of one?

We entered the treatment room. She handed me a lengthy list of options.

"Please choose shape," she said.

I glanced down. The list was headed by the proverbial Brazilian wax, also known as the "Playboy," it informed me, followed by variations on the theme, including the Crotch Crop, the Muff Mold, the Snatch Slash, the Slit Snip and the Clit Clip. Each one was extravagantly described in florid prose, like the menu items at those pompous bistros frequented by the snob mob.

"I don't want anything fancy," I said tersely. "Just the basics."

She straightened herself up to her full four foot eight and raised her prominent nose in the air.

"As you wish," she replied.

Guess I wasn't brazen enough to suit her artistic sensibilities.

She handed me a pair of paper panties the size of a postage stamp.

"Take off everything, put this on, lie down," she said tightly. "I go heat vex."

She left the room. I disrobed and pulled on the skimpy skivvies. Might as well not have bothered.

I was about to lie down on the torture rack when

the thought struck me—for once, I was alone in a room where I could actually do some snooping.

I looked around the small room. A corner shelf held some towels, some lotions, and…an index card file. I sprung open the lid. It was full of cards organized by alphabetical dividers. A client file! So, old-world Marushka hadn't gone digital.

I quickly flipped to the *W*'s. There it was—Tricia Weinstein's client information. It contained her name, address, phone number and her waxing shape preferences. She was partial to bunny ears.

Whoa! A sudden dizzy spell came over me. I'd been hit with TMI—too much information.

On the other hand, it was too little. This didn't really give me any meaningful insight into the woman. But wait, what was this? A section at the bottom of the card was labeled Comments. Underneath that was a scribbled note: "Careful of caesarean scar." What on earth?

I heard a shuffling outside the room. Marushka was approaching, armed with hot wax.

I hurriedly slipped the card back in, snapped the lid shut and climbed onto the table just as the door opened.

I lay there, staring up at the ceiling, baffled. Why

would Tricia have a caesarean scar? She had told me
her pregnancy was her first one. Had she been lying?
Had she had a child in the past that she didn't want
anyone to know about? If so, could this have anything
to do with Gladys?

I was so preoccupied with these thoughts that I
hardly noticed as Marushka applied the wax, topped it
with linen strips and then savagely yanked my hair out.

CHAPTER 19

After leaving Marushka's, now a hair-free Harriet, I considered what I'd found out about Tricia. What had seemed like a momentous discovery back there in the harrowing confines of the torture chamber now appeared insignificant under less hair-raising circumstances.

So what if Tricia Weinstein had a caesarean scar? So she'd had a baby in her past that she wanted to keep in the past. Granted, this was the twenty-first century and single mothers were no longer branded with a scarlet letter A, but for someone like Tricia, whose entire *raison d'être* derived from maintaining an image of perfection, having had a baby and possibly given it up for adoption would probably be viewed as a failure, and hence something to be kept under wraps. In any case, I couldn't see what it would have to do with the death of her housekeeper. Surely

Gladys hadn't discovered Tricia's deep dark secret and threatened to reveal it…or had she?

I decided I needed to let that thought percolate in my brain for a while to come up with an effective way to follow up on that possibility. In the meantime, I decided to pursue another angle—the truck accident that had killed sixteen Mayan workers shortly before Gladys disappeared. I had to explore the possibility that Gladys had known something about the accident and had been put out of the way.

There was only one known witness to the accident, and that was the sole survivor—the truck driver. If the crash really hadn't been an accident but something more sinister, then the driver would be the player with the most obvious incentive for eliminating another witness.

As I'd done with Mark Cohen, I decided to pay a surprise visit to the suspect. Okay, so maybe that strategy hadn't worked so well before, but why should that stop me now?

I rode to my office, where I took out my file on the case and found the newspaper article that I'd printed off the Web. It reported the driver as one George Rodgers of Briny Breezes. I locked up the office, got on my Hog and rode over to the man's home.

Briny Breezes is one of the strangest places on earth. It's a tiny municipality that takes up a quarter-mile stretch of prime oceanfront real estate, wedged between the ritzy enclaves of Ocean Ridge and Gulf Stream. So what's strange about that, you ask? Here's what: Briny Breezes is a trailer park.

Don't ask me how that happened. I don't know. Don't ask me how the place has managed not to be bought out by the developers that swarm Florida like flies. And don't ask me how you get to be a resident there.

I roared down the main drag of Briny Breezes—all four blocks of it—to where it ended, then turned right a block to Rodgers's place. The front porch had a hell of a view of the Atlantic, if you could actually sit on the porch, that is, which you couldn't, because it sagged at a thirty-degree angle. Most of its floorboards were rotted out, and it looked to be in imminent danger of collapse.

A license plate tacked up next to the front door assured me that the trailer's registration was up to date. Well, that made me feel a whole lot better.

I walked up a makeshift ramp and knocked on the screen door, which hung askew off one hinge. I waited a minute, watching a row of sandpipers run into shore and back out again, following the ocean waves. When no one answered, I knocked again.

"Hold yer horses!" a voice came from within. "I'm comin'! My legs ain't what they used to be, ya know."

The door behind the screen opened inward. I peered in. There was no one there. Oh, great. Some P.I.s get to deal with haunted mansions; I get haunted mobile homes.

"Well?" a voice demanded from the region of my pelvis.

I looked down. I was looking at a guy in his forties, sporting a long gray beard and long gray hair. He was in a wheelchair. Where his legs used to be, there were now stumps.

"Mr. Rodgers?" I asked.

"You're lookin' at him—what's left of him." He gave a throaty laugh that devolved into a coughing spasm.

When he'd recovered, I said, "My name is Harriet Horowitz. I'm a private investigator looking into the death of a young Guatemalan woman out in the tomato fields. Would you mind if I ask you a few questions?"

"What's this got to do with me?" he asked.

"She was killed a few days after your truck accident. I was wondering if there might be a connection."

He laughed and coughed again. "As you can plainly see, honey, I weren't in no shape to be killin' nobody after the accident. So you can cross me right off your list of suspects."

Well, he had a point there.

"Would you mind telling me about the accident?" I asked.

"Ain't much to tell. But hell, come on in." He wheeled his chair back from the door. I entered a dark, fake-wood-paneled living room. A window air-conditioning unit wheezed in the background. The furnishings consisted of a seventies-era TV complete with rabbit ears, a plaid couch strategically held together with duct tape and a chipped coffee table bearing an ashtray overflowing with butts. The decor consisted of a series of studio portraits beginning with an infant, who transformed into a little girl, then a young lady and finally a high school graduate in a cap and gown. My keen investigative acumen led me to deduce that she was Rodgers's daughter.

"Take a load off," Rodgers said, motioning to the couch. I sat down. My ass sank practically to the floor. A spring poked me in a most unfortunate part of my anatomy.

"Getcha a beer or coffee or somethin'?" he asked.

"No, thanks," I replied. "So what can you tell me about the accident?"

"All's I can tell you is what I tol' the po-lice. I don't remember nothin' about it. I was haulin' a bunch o' them workers down from Boynton for the day. It was foggy. I couldn't see much. Next thing I knowed, I'm lyin' in a hospital bed and I cain't feel my legs. I look down, and they ain't there.

"When they tol' me all them workers was kilt, well, I jes' about like to curl up an' die right then and there. Hell, I ain't never give a hoot about a bunch o' illegals, but when it come right down to it, them sixteen dead souls weighed right heavy on my conscience. Only thing kept me goin' was my baby girl." He nodded at the photos lining the wall.

"Her mama done left us when she was no more 'an a tyke. Went an' got her one o' them sex-change operations. Whatchamacall them people nowadays? Transgentile?"

"Transgender," I supplied.

"Yeah, whatever. Got her titties lopped off an' all. Come to think of it, we'd make a pretty good matched set now." He laughed and coughed. "Anyways, it's jes' been me and my little girl all these years.

She's all growed up now, goin' to the state college over to Tallahassee. Got herself a full scholarship, done her ol' man real proud."

There was a scratching at the door, the sound of a key being inserted into the lock.

"That'll be Wanda," Rodgers said. "My home health aide. Comes by to help me out ever' day 'bout this time."

The door opened and a woman entered. Long frizzy black hair framed her pale face. Her eyes peered out from behind a pair of large, thick glasses. A set of baggy hospital scrubs drooped over her plump physique. This was not a Boca Babe.

"Hey, George," she said.

"Hey, Wanda," he replied.

She looked at me. "Ready for your bath?" she asked. I was about to take offense before I realized she was addressing Rodgers.

"Yeah, in a minute," he replied. "We was just finishin' up here. There's a fresh pot of coffee in the kitchen. Help yourself."

"Okay." She went through an open doorway into the tiny kitchenette.

"Oh, by the way," she called across the counter that separated the two rooms, "those old cars we were talkin' about? I talked to my dealer friend and he says he's had some good inventory come in, so he oughta be able to fix you up with something."

"Thanks, hon," George said. "Been on the lookout for a used vehicle since my engine give out a couple weeks ago," he explained to me.

Hmm, that seemed odd. How could he drive? Guess he must have had the car adapted with hand controls.

"Yeah," I said, "well, look, I'm not going to keep you. So basically, you're telling me that you have no idea what caused your accident?"

"Yep, that's the long and short of it. The cops said they thought something must've sprung up in the road right in front of the truck. An animal maybe. There's them Florida panthers out there once in a blue moon. Or it coulda been a car pulled out in front o' me suddenly. They said I just swerved off the road real sudden, no skid marks or nothin'. Well, whatever it was was long gone by the time the cops got to the scene. And yeah, before you ask, there wasn't no alcohol or drugs involved. You can bet your bippy they tested me. No way—I do my drinking strictly on my own time. 'Course, I got me plenty o' that now!" Another laugh and cough.

"And there were no witnesses that you're aware of?"

"Nope."

"Okay," I said. "Thanks for your time."

I rose from the couch. Or, I attempted to rise. I made it a couple inches but was sucked right back in. I tried again, this time using my arms to push off. Same result. Damn—this couch was the Black Hole of Briny Breezes. No light could escape, much less my ass.

I finally made it on the third try. Man, this was embarrassing. A Krav Maga mistress KO'd by a Killer Couch. Ouch!

"Yeah, so, as I was saying, if you think of anything else, give me a call." I dug one of my cards out of my back pocket and handed it to him.

"All right, hon," he said.

I walked out the door, the screen slamming behind me. I took a step onto the porch and my foot got stuck in one of the spaces between the floorboards. I dragged my foot out, got on my Hog and roared off with as much dignity as I could muster.

Later that afternoon, I headed over to the Krav Maga center.

I'd actually been avoiding the place for the past couple days, ever since my dream about Lior. In truth,

I was kind of embarrassed to see him, even though, of course, he didn't know anything about the dream. Nonetheless, I felt as if he'd see right through me, all the way down to my hot red bra and thong set, which, of course, I don't wear for anyone's pleasure but my own. Like I said before, some habits die hard.

So in class that day, I studiously avoided his gaze. But it was impossible to avoid his hands gripping my arms, his thighs brushing against mine, his breath on my neck. Krav Maga is, after all, about bare-handed contact combat. But that day it seemed more like barely contained combustion.

As soon as class was over, I bolted for the door. I had just about made my escape when I felt Lior's hand on my shoulder.

"What's your rush, slick chick?" he asked.

I turned. My head was level with his massive shoulders.

"I'm a busy beaver," I said. Whoops, maybe that wasn't the best choice of words. I sneaked a look up at him. Amusement glinted in his black eyes. I quickly averted my gaze. Whoops, that was a mistake, too. The kind of glance that could be taken as a come-on.

What the hell was wrong with me? I was Dirty Harriet, not a flirty coquette. A gumptious gumshoe, not a goo-goo eyed girl. The last thing I needed in my life was a sexual distraction, especially with a strutting South Beach club king who actually used terms like *slick chick* and *foxy lady*. Please. But he sure did have a great set of pecs, not to mention a great set of buns.... Oh, hell.

"You know," Lior was saying, "the gun club is having that mixed-doubles shooting competition coming up. I was thinking we'd make a great team. What do you say?"

Say what? Was this some new tack he was trying to hook up with me?

Lior and I were both regulars at the local shooting range. But it's not like we'd ever gone there *together*. I had taken up shooting back in the precontemplation stage of my recovery. I was on my way to breaking out of my Boca Babe prison, although I didn't know that yet. But a definite sense of unease had started to creep in. For one thing, I was getting real sick of spending my days buying up Gucci for my poochie. So I traded in my shopping addiction for a shooting addiction. And yeah, I'd become a damn good shot. After all, you didn't think that gunning down my husband had been just plain dumb luck, did you?

But the idea of teaming up with Lior was, well, it

was tempting. Too tempting. I mean, shooting together meant sharing together, and who knew where that could lead? I couldn't take the risk. Or could I?

"I'll think about it. See ya later," I muttered to his chest and bailed.

"It'll be my pleasure," he called after me.

I rode home and spent a quiet evening with Lana, trying not too successfully to banish Lior from my mind. I finally gave up and went to bed.

Late that night, I was awakened from a sound sleep by the phone ringing.

"Yeah," I mumbled.

"Rodgers here," the voice at the other end said. I was instantly awake.

"Been thinkin' 'bout our talk today," he went on. His words had that slow, deliberate quality characteristic of the habitually inebriated. "You said to call you if I thought of anything. I did, so I am."

"What is it?"

"Reckon we'd best discuss this in person. Don't put no stock in them cellular thingamajigs. Somebody might be a-listenin' in."

Great. It was two o'clock in the morning and I was talking to a paranoid drunk. Who said a P.I.'s life isn't glamorous?

"All right," I said. "When can you meet?"

"Reckon now's as good a time as any."

"Man, it's 2:00 a.m.!" I cried.

"Yep," came the reply.

I could see there was no reasoning with him. Besides, I was wide awake now, my curiosity piqued.

"I'll meet you in an hour," I said.

CHAPTER 20

I got out of my warm, cozy bed and put on my leggings, tank top and leathers. I boarded my boat, put on my earplugs and earmuffs, and took off into the night. It was eerie in the Everglades in this witching hour. Only a sliver of moon lit my way as the saw grass whipped past me. An occasional owl hooted.

I arrived on land, then rode my Hog the twenty miles to the beach. I turned north on A1A. Out on the ocean, I could hear a storm brewing. Powerful waves slammed the shore, eating away at the land as they sucked mouthfuls of sand back out with them.

I pulled up to Rodgers's trailer. The porch was still sagging and the screen door was still hanging by a thread. I knocked on the door and waited a couple minutes. No answer. I tried again. Still nothing. Now I was getting seriously irritated. Rodgers had summoned me out of my warm and cozy bed to come out here on this godforsaken night. If he'd decided to go out in the meantime, I'd be real pissed.

I opened the screen and pushed on the door. It swung open.

"Rodgers!" I called. Nothing. I stepped inside. He was sprawled out on the killer couch, snoring. Beer bottles littered the floor around him. I walked over and shoved him on the shoulder.

"Yo! Wake up, bud!"

He snorted, but didn't budge. "Hey!" I yelled. I shook his shoulders. No response. Shit. The man was passed out in a drunken stupor.

I opened his eyelids. His eyes were rolled back in his head. Not a good sign. I felt the pulse in his throat. It was about twenty beats a minute. A real bad sign. The guy was knocking on heaven's door. Damn! As if I didn't have enough troubles of my own.

I got out my cell and called 911. The ambulance arrived a few minutes later, siren blaring. Naturally, the entire population of Briny Breezes came out on their sagging porches to check out the excitement. Two paramedics trooped in and proceeded to do their thing. They and their equipment took up just about all the room. I stayed back in a corner, watching.

They put an oxygen mask on him, then gave him a shot of adrenaline.

"What's he on?" one of the paramedics asked me.

"I don't know. Beer, I guess," I said, indicating the empty bottles.

"This isn't just a beer buzz," he said.

The other paramedic began looking around the room. He went into the kitchen and opened drawers.

"Okay, here we go," he said, holding up a plastic baggie containing a few white, oval-shaped pills.

"Old cars," he said. The other one grunted.

"Old cars? What are you talking about?" I asked.

"Lady, what rock have you been living under? Old cars—that's the street name for OxyContin. The latest and greatest substance of choice." He rolled his eyes. "We got us an OD on downers."

So Wanda, Rodgers's health care aide, was his supplier. She'd been talking about "old cars" the last time I'd been here. How was I supposed to know that was code for O.C., OxyContin, the widely abused narcotic painkiller? What other clues had I missed in this whole investigation?

Rodgers's eyes fluttered open. I walked over and laid a hand on his arm. "Hey," I said softly, "it's Harriet Horowitz."

"What you doin' here?" he asked.

"You asked me to come, remember?"

"Oh, yeah."

"Ma'am, please step back," one of the paramedics said. "We need to get him to the hospital." I did as instructed and they loaded him onto a stretcher. I followed them out the door. Damned if I'd come out here in the middle of the night for nothing.

They loaded him onto the ambulance, the eyes of Briny Breezes watching every move. I climbed in after him, the paramedics making no protest. One of them stayed in the back, the other went up front to drive. We got rolling.

"Rodgers," I said, "what was it you wanted to tell me? About your accident?"

His eyes opened briefly, then shut again.

"Accident," he mumbled. "Yeah. I seen what happened." His speech was labored, muted. I leaned in closer.

"Lamont…pesticide," he gasped.

"Jake Lamont? The crew boss?" I asked.

"Yeah."

"What about pesticide?"

"Spilled…on the road."

"Lamont spilled some pesticide on the road?"

He nodded.

"Why?"

"Banned substance...had to get rid of it...EPA coming down...surprise visit...must've been tipped off."

"So he poured it on the road and your truck slid on it?"

"Yeah, I seen him do it...I hit that slimy stuff and wham! Nothin' I could do."

"Why didn't you tell this to the police?"

"Couldn't...in hospital...had visit from corporate honchos...convinced me to keep quiet...said they'd pay all my medical bills and disability, take care of my little girl. Had to think about my baby—no one else around to watch out for her. Had to do it—for my baby girl."

So Rodgers had been paid off by Big Tomato to keep silent about illegal dumping of a banned pesticide. Had Gladys known something about this, too, and been permanently silenced?

"What about Gladys, the dead Mayan woman?" I asked him.

"She was there. Sittin' out in the tomato fields. Waitin' for that boyfriend o' hers, I guess. I seen 'em out there some mornin's when I made that run. She was there that mornin', must've seen the whole thing go down."

So there I had it at last—a clear motive for Gladys's murder. She'd been done in by Lamont or some other Big Tomato hatchet man. I felt sick to my stomach.

Suddenly Rodgers's hand shot out and gripped my forearm.

"After you come by this afternoon…conscience got to me… It just ain't right, what they done to me an' them sixteen poor suckers… It just ain't right." He took a deep breath. "Anyways, my baby's growed up an' gone now…so's I'm free to talk. They got nothin' on me now…I'm free."

Then his eyes rolled back in his head and his breathing became rapid and shallow.

"Damn!" the paramedic exclaimed. "He's going into respiratory arrest. Step back!"

CHAPTER 21

The paramedic started performing CPR. He kept at it…and at it…and at it. Minutes passed as the ambulance tore through the deserted streets, siren wailing. Finally the vehicle came to a stop and the siren went silent. The doors opened. The paramedic stopped his efforts, taking deep breaths of his own, sweat dripping down his face. The stretcher was pulled out. I climbed out and watched as the paramedics wheeled Rodgers through the doors of the E.R. There was nothing more I could get from him or do for him.

I got a cab ride back out to the trailer park to pick up my bike. I rode to my office and spent the rest of the morning and the early afternoon catching up on my other cases. I busted one lowlife who was scamming Boca retirees with phantom discount charter flights to New York to visit their grandkids, and another sewer rat who was conning underage girls into posing for nude photos with promises of big-time modeling contracts. All in a day's work.

But my thoughts kept going back to Rodgers. Around noon I decided to call the hospital to check on his condition. When I started getting the runaround, I started to suspect that the news wasn't good. Finally a doctor came on the line and confirmed my fears: Rodgers had died that morning, a few hours after arrival.

A stab of guilt passed through me. Would Rodgers have OD'd had it not been for my probing questions? Yeah, I'd gotten some answers. But could I afford the price?

Sighing, I called the contessa to give her the latest. As we talked, a thought struck me.

"What if Rodgers's OD was no accident?" I posed. "What if he was shut up by Big Tomato? That would mean the Corporate Corruption Division knew he'd squealed."

"How would they know?" the contessa asked.

"As far as I can see, there's only one way—from Wanda, the health worker who was there when I was asking Rodgers about the truck accident. She might actually be a plant."

"Well, it looks like a chat with Wanda is in order," said the contessa.

"Right," I replied. If I could establish that Rodgers was a victim of homicide by a corporate hired hand, that would strengthen the case for Gladys being a victim of the same.

I had no idea where to find Wanda, but I figured she'd be back to Rodgers's place at her usual time that afternoon, either to provide her usual services or to see whether her intentional OD had done its job. So, I'd go back and lie in wait. I headed out to the trailer park.

I hadn't locked Rodgers's door behind us when I left with the paramedics that morning. I walked in and quickly scoped out the place. I decided to bide my time in a broom closet and observe Wanda's actions when she came in. I stepped into the closet and looked out through the slats in the louvered door.

Ten minutes later, Wanda walked in.

"Hey, George," she yelled. Receiving no response, she repeated herself. Then she did a quick walk through the trailer.

She took out her cell phone and made a call.

"It's Wanda," she said. "My one o'clock isn't here…I don't know…yeah, okay…you want the report on my twelve o'clock? Yeah, Mrs. Blumfeld. BP ninety over sixty, temperature 97.6, pulse a hundred

and two. I emptied her Foley, did her sponge bath...
yeah, okay. Bye."

Well, there was nothing sinister there. Sounded
like Wanda was just reporting to her employer.

I heard her go into the kitchen and open a cabinet.
There was some rattling around. It became more and
more frantic.

"Shit," she said. "Where's the stash?"

Then she placed another call.

"This is Wanda. One of our customers is missing
and so's his candy. Of course, I looked. That's the first
thing I thought of, resale. No, I don't know where he
is."

I figured this was an opportune time to announce
my presence.

"He's dead," I said, coming out of the closet.

Wanda's eyes bulged as her face turned a whiter
shade of pale. She let out a bloodcurdling scream
and dropped the phone.

Gee, I just love making an impression on folks.

"What...what are you doing here?" she sputtered.
"What do you mean, George is dead?"

"OD'd," I said. "On OxyContin and booze. Now,
you wouldn't know anything about that, would you?"

"What are you talking about?"

"How does a murder rap grab you?" I asked.

She staggered backward. Her calves struck the Killer Couch and she went down into that bottomless pit. She lay there, flailing.

"I'll tell you what," I said. "How about you let me know whose payroll you're on, and maybe I just might forget to mention your little retail business to the cops."

"Payroll? My Brother's Keeper Home Health Care. And I resent your implication. I'm a healer, not a dealer."

Well, what do you know. Wanda had a way with words.

"You read the paper, right?" she continued. "About the high cost of prescription drugs for seniors and the disabled? I provide a desperately needed service to the community—priced-right prescriptions."

"Yeah," I said. "Let me guess. You palm leftover pills from your patients who don't know any better or have kicked the bucket, then resell them to others. Gosh, you could be turning a profit on one little pill four or five times over."

She glared at me. "Hey, who appointed you to the morality militia? I don't have to put up with you."

Right. And I didn't have to put up with her. I turned my back and headed for the door.

I heard her huffing and puffing, struggling to get off the Killer Couch.

"Hey! You can't just leave me here like this. I'm stuck here! Come back!"

"So sorry you've fallen and can't get up. Why don't you try calling a forklift company?" I threw over my shoulder as the screen door slammed behind me.

"I can't reach my phone! Get your ass back here!"

I stood out on the porch for a while, listening to Wanda's screams. It was a hot one today. I took off my boots and walked on the sand to the water's edge. The ocean waves washed over my bare feet. If only they could wash away my guilt over Rodgers's death.

It was looking like an accident or a suicide. Based on her actions and words, Wanda didn't seem to have a clue about any Big Tomato connection. Apparently, she was just a small-time independent operator, not a hired hit woman. Still, even if the corporation hadn't knocked off Rodgers, that didn't mean it hadn't done Gladys. But how the hell would I find out?

CHAPTER 22

I needed to get inside Big Tomato and find out what was going on in there. So the next morning at the office, I logged on to the Web and found the name of the corporation, Consolidated Tomato Growers of Palm Beach County, and its CEO, Zachariah J. Zachariah. Then I picked up the phone.

"This is Brenda Lee Harper with Au Naturelle Cosmetique," I drawled in my best Southern-belle imitation. "We are interested in bulk purchase of tomatoes for use in our line of fine products for the visage. I wonder if I might make an appointment with Mr. Zachariah to discuss the potential for our companies to enter into a mutually beneficial business arrangement?"

"One moment please, let me check his calendar," the receptionist said, putting me on hold. She came back a couple minutes later. "Yes, Ms. Harper, Mr. Zachariah would be delighted to meet with you at three o'clock this afternoon if that's suitable."

"That's wonderful, darlin'. I'll see y'all then."

I went over to my office closet and took out the one item of apparel that remained from my Boca Babe life. It was a white Dolce & Gabbana suit, together with matching four-inch vamp shoes, which I kept strictly for undercover operations such as this. Then I reached way into the back of my bottom desk drawer and pulled out my secret stash—a Ziploc bag filled with the finest cosmetics money can buy— again, remnants of my past life. The only thing missing was the jewelry. As a Boca Babe, I'd had diamond studs practically soldered into my earlobes. But I had few regrets about living gem-free. After dusting my husband, I'd dusted off all my rocks and sold them to buy my Hog.

I pulled out a sheet of perforated card stock, spent a few minutes on the computer and printed out a snazzy business card to confirm my new identity. The phone number and e-mail address, were, of course, bogus. I was ready to roll.

I loaded the suit, the shoes and the greasepaint into my saddlebags. Having to haul all my shit around like this was damn inconvenient. As I packed, I started to miss my days as a Boca Babe when all I'd carried was a miniature Gucci backpack to hold my mirror, credit cards and cell phone. But then I reminded myself that letting myself get knocked around just to keep from having to carry knockoffs had been considerably more inconvenient.

I rode up to the company's headquarters in West Palm. The offices were located in a tall, sparkling glass building on Flagler Drive, overlooking Lake Worth and the gilded isle of Palm Beach beyond. I spotted a Starbucks nearby. I went into the restroom and emerged minutes later as a Southern belle on steroids.

I teetered across the parking lot, entered the building and rode the elevator to the top. In short order, I was seated in a luxury office suite, sipping gourmet coffee and looking across a desk at a fifty-something suit.

"Ms. Harper, I'm delighted to make your acquaintance," he said. "How may I be of assistance?"

"Well, Mr. Zachariah," I drawled. "My company has developed a revolutionary new proprietary line of lipsticks and blushes that rely on a tomato base. You see, at Au Naturelle Cosmetique, our products are one-hundred percent synthetic-free, animal product-free and allergen-free. The only thing that's not free is the price. No doubt, y'all can appreciate the importance of quality to discerning clientele. Our customers are connoisseurs of natural beauty, as well as champions of the preservation of this beautiful blue-green planet that we all share. As such, price is no object to our devoted consumers.

"Now, our new tomato-based products yield long-lasting pigmentation to the lips and cheeks. In addition, their intrinsic Vitamin C provides exfoliating and rejuvenating properties. All this with no harm to the planet and all its myriad creatures. In short, Mr. Zachariah, it's truly a miracle product, and we are poised to become the world's leading cosmetics concern. Between y'all and me, we'll have Dior, La Prairie, Clarins all running for cover.

"Now here's the thing, Mr. Zachariah. We require a very significant and steady supply of tomatoes. My product developers inform me that one lipstick will require the juice of forty-three tomatoes. So, y'all do the math."

I paused for effect. I could see the wheels turning in his head. They weren't turning fast enough, so I helped him out.

"Bottom line, Mr. Zachariah, we will need several million tons of tomatoes per year."

The man was practically coming in his pants at the prospect.

"So," I continued, "I am contacting every tomato growers' association in the country to see who might be able to provide us with the most favorable terms."

He licked his lips. "Ms. Harper, I will get my people right on it. We'll have a proposal to you by the end of the week. I can assure you that you will find it to be most attractive."

"That's lovely. Now, y'all understand, of course, that we must have strict assurance that your growing practices in no way endanger our natural environment, nor exploit any resources, be they animal, vegetable, mineral or human. As I said, our customers are aesthetically aware, as well as environmentally enlightened. They simply will not abide any abusive business practices whatsoever."

"Ms. Harper, we are a match made in heaven. Our affiliated growers are committed to the highest environmental and ethical standards in the tomato industry."

Yeah, right.

"I'll be happy to take you on a tour of our fields. You will find that our worker housing facilities are the best in the country—clean, modern, comfortable. We provide on-site recreational facilities, too. You see, it's really very simple. We believe a happy worker is a productive worker."

Just when you think you've heard it all. So Big Tomato had some bogus model housing someplace that they showed off to visitors, not letting them see the actual shacks they kept the slaves in.

"Why sure, Mr. Zachariah, I'll have my assistant check my schedule and get back to you on that."

"We can also supply you with all our environmental impact assessments that have been filed with the EPA. Of course, as you probably know, all that data is available through the Freedom of Information Act, but what with government bureaucracy being what it is, who has the time to jump through those hoops?"

Well, that was a smooth move. I had to give him credit for his preemptive strike. Big Tomato must have someone inside the EPA who fixed the reports. Probably the same person who had tipped them off about the impending EPA visit on the day of the truck accident.

Shit. I wasn't making much headway here. If Big Tomato had silenced Gladys and if this guy knew about it, he sure wasn't letting anything slip. And if I couldn't get it from him, how could I get it? It wasn't as if they would have left some tangible record of payoffs, bumpoffs and whatever other nefarious activities they were engaged in. If they had really killed

Gladys, it looked as if they'd committed the perfect murder.

"All right, Mr. Zachariah," I said. "I look forward to receiving your proposal. And I'll have my assistant get in touch about that field visit. So long now."

I stood up and shook his hand. He walked me to the elevator, oozing false charm the whole way. It set my teeth on edge, like when you bite into a piece of aluminum.

At last the elevator came and I made my escape. When the doors closed, I leaned back against the wall and let out a long breath.

This situation was reprehensible. These slimeball slaveowners were polluting my beloved Florida, causing fatal accidents, dispensing hush money and greasing palms, all with impunity. But what pissed me off more than anything was that I'd put on high heels and makeup for this.

The elevator doors opened and I stepped out. I teetered back over to my Hog and pulled my clothes and a supersize bottle of Xtreme Makeup Remover out of the saddlebags. I reentered the Starbucks.

I reemerged as my true authentic self. Maybe Brenda the Southern belle was beat, but Dirty Harriet was unbeatable. I was back and badder than ever.

There were still avenues to explore, leads to follow.
I would nail Gladys's killer yet.

I roared off in a cloud of dust.

CHAPTER 23

Saturday morning, I chilled out with a little motor-cycle maintenance. As I was checking the air pressure on the tires, I got to thinking about what Lupe had said about my parental problem. Despite my earlier protests, her words kept gnawing at me. Could she be right? Was I an overbearing control freak when it came to Mom and her love life? Well…okay, maybe Lupe had a point.

I decided to back off and let Mom make her own romantic blunders. What could I really do besides make a fool of myself if I made a scene about Leonard Goldblatt? If I interfered, I would only alienate her. Was that what I really wanted? Once she was married to that weasel and realized that he was only after her money, that's when she'd need me most. If I alienated her now, I'd be abandoning her in her time of need. So, I would grit my teeth and greet Mom as she came off the plank when the *Merry Mermaid* sailed into

Fort Lauderdale Tuesday night. And I wouldn't say a word about her fleecing future fiancé.

Feeling pretty virtuous, I headed out to the beach party. It was to be an all-day affair with a barbecue, swimming and beach games. Of course, there was no way I'd last that long. A couple hours of socializing was about all I could take before my need for solitude reasserted itself with a vengeance.

I arrived at the beachfront park and parked my Hog in a secluded corner of the lot underneath a sprawling banyan tree. I didn't want to attract a throng of gawking beachgoers oohing and aahing over the bike. My Hog doesn't have any customized touches. It's just your basic no-frills, clean-lined Hugger, meaning it hugs the ground. A classic Harley. And that draws attention. That day, I didn't want to keep an eye on it, and I didn't want to be distracted from my intended task of interviewing Gladys's women friends.

With Lupe's help, I tried to talk to several of the Mayan women, but they consistently denied knowing anything that could shed light on the murder. I was starting to think that there was a conspiracy of silence. No one ever gets killed without somebody somewhere knowing something, and of course that somebody is often a close associate of the victim. What were these women hiding? And how could I get them to give it up?

Lacking any plan of action at the moment, I decided I might as well enjoy the beach, having gone through the waxing ordeal just so I could put on my swimsuit. After all, when would that happen again? So I took off my shorts and tank top, revealing my black bikini and the rose tattoo on my left boob. The tattoo actually predates my biking days. I'd gotten it around the time it started to dawn on me that my marriage itself wasn't coming up roses. They say there's a hidden Harley gene inside everyone, and I guess that tattoo was an early sign that my recessive trait was ready to break out and become dominant.

I waded into the ocean and swam out fifty yards or so, then turned and stroked parallel to the shore for about a half mile and back. I emerged just as preparations were underway for a picnic lunch. Lupe was grilling some jalapeño burgers. She pulled a small purple velvet bag out of her cleavage, opened it and tossed the contents onto the coals.

"What's that?" I asked.

"Juniper berries. They bring protection and health." Then she intoned, "With this seasoning I empower the energy of this glorious hour. As we eat this magic meal, the power of this spell will heal."

Then the entertainment commenced, in the form of the Three Wise Men—Lupe's brothers, Balthasar, Gaspar and Melchior—who, as it happened, comprised a band of strolling mariachi singers. I will say that the sight and sound of three hulking *hombres* dressed like matadors, wearing black sombreros and standing barefoot in the surf while playing a violin, a guitar and a trumpet, was a little unusual.

The bizarro effect was heightened by the appearance of the contessa, who showed up dragging along her own custom lounge chair, umbrella and a little doggie tent for Coco. She sat there, looking out to sea and sipping a Long Island iced tea.

Lupe and I laid out a blanket beside her and sat down to eat. Just as we were finishing a dessert of *tres leches*, I noticed a latecomer to the group. It was Eulalia. She was staying off to the side, away from the others. She had her arms clasped around herself as if she were cold. She wasn't eating, and she looked kind of pale.

"Look at Eulalia," I said.

"Yeah, she doesn't look well," Lupe said. "Let's go see if she's all right."

We walked over and sat down on either side of her. Up close, she looked even worse. Her skin was clammy and her eyes were glassy. Lupe spoke to her, but Eulalia kept throwing nervous glances at the Mayan men, who were tossing a ball around nearby. A couple times she opened her mouth as if she were on the verge of saying something, but then apparently she changed her mind. Lupe and I looked at each other in frustration. Here was a sick woman who obviously wanted to tell us something.

Well, there was no way to shake it out of her. Damn it, this case was really exasperating.

By then, I'd surpassed my two-hour socialization-tolerance limit, so it was time for me to retreat back to my hermitage. I said my goodbyes and walked back to my bike to the strains of "La Cucaracha."

As I rode out of the park, I found Eulalia's demeanor still bothering me. Now I was sure that she and the other Mayan women were hiding something, and the men were the reason for their silence. Besides that, I was really worried about her health.

I was consumed with these thoughts as I slowly drove west, away from the beach. Just a couple blocks from the ocean, traffic piled up. Great. I was stuck in a traffic jam. We crawled along at a stop-and-go pace.

I sat there for a good twenty minutes, alternating between idling and creeping. Needless to say, several morons thought that things would speed up if they honked their horns, all together at once, of course.

Okay, beam me up, Scotty, Hog and all.

Finally, we reached the cause of the backup. A minor fender bender on the side of the road. As I passed by, I felt a wave of irritation. After all, if you're going to be stuck in traffic for so long, you want at least a spectacular sight of mangled and twisted metal to gape at as the payoff for the wait.

Immediately past the accident site, the traffic lightened up. At last! I opened up the throttle and accelerated.

Suddenly, there was a horrible grinding and clashing noise. What the hell?

The Hog started skidding. Something was seriously wrong.

I pulled in on the clutch to disengage the gears. That didn't help. I was still skidding. Shit! The wheels were locked up. What was going on?

The bike was now sliding out from under me. I shifted my weight to correct for the imbalance, but it was no use. I was down.

I hit the ground on my right side and was dragged

along a few feet by the momentum. I could feel the asphalt trying to burn through my leathers. My helmet scraped along. It sounded like thunder.

After what seemed like hours, the bike and I finally came to a stop.

I heard screeching brakes behind me and then I was surrounded by faces peering down at me. Voices assailed me from all sides.

"Are you all right?"

"Take it easy."

"Don't get up too fast."

I took off my helmet and looked around, dazed. After a while, things came into focus. I mentally went through an inventory of my limbs. I could feel them all. Okay, I was still in one piece. Nothing seemed to be severed, broken or punctured.

I got up slowly, then walked over to the bike, which had come to rest a few feet away from me. I looked down and saw what had happened: most of the spokes on both wheels had come loose, lodging in the wheel rims, the frame and the engine.

I knew immediately there was only one way this could have happened: sabotage. Chuck had been right—someone was out to get me.

CHAPTER 24

The police came and took an accident report. When they saw that it was a crime scene, a whole new set of paperwork was required. They promised to investigate, but I wasn't holding my breath that they would nail the perp. I'd learned long ago that I was on my own when it came to assaults on me.

The paramedics arrived, determined that I had no obvious signs of injury, then argued with me over whether I should go to the hospital. In the end, I won with a promise to get myself checked out if I began to feel worse. I don't think they were holding their breaths, either.

Then I had to do it again—call Chuck to come rescue my ass.

"Chuckles!" I yelled into the phone. "I rode to the coast and now I'm toast! My spokes are smoked! My ride is fried!"

"What in hell do you think you are, a rap artist?"

he snorted. "Darlin', bag the rhymes. You're wastin' your time. You ain't no poet and you know it. Now, where are you?"

I told him and twenty minutes later he pulled up in the flatbed.

"We gotta stop meeting like this," he said.

"Yeah, tongues might start wagging," I agreed.

We went through the routine again, loading the bike onto the flatbed, Chuck warning me to be on guard, urging me to come stay with him and Enrique that night, and me insisting that I just wanted to be home alone. So again he dropped me off at the edge of the swamp.

He headed back on solid ground and I hovered off into the quagmire.

I arrived at the cabin, docked the boat and went in. Man, this was one time I wished I had a bathtub. A long hot soak would be just the ticket right now. Maybe I could get a Jacuzzi installed out here one of these days.

Oh, shit! That kind of thinking was a warning sign of potential relapse into Babeness. "Stinkin' Thinkin'" as AA calls it. I needed to nip this in the bud, right here and now. It was time for some relapse prevention, and, of course, a substitute vice was the solution.

I took a quick shower, then poured three fingers of Hennessy into my crystal glass and sat in my rocking chair. I looked around for my recovery sponsor, Lana. There she was, hind legs and tail submerged, front legs and snout resting on a piece of driftwood.

"I want my Jacuzzi!" I whined.

"Yeah, and I want my MTV," she replied in my mind. "You know it starts with just that one slip," she went on. "First it's the Jacuzzi, then it's the swimming pool, then it's the home theater…before you know it, you're back in the Babe Badlands. You don't wanna go there."

"You're right, I don't. But I'm so tempted. I've had one shitty day."

"Would you rather have a shitty day as a free woman, or would you rather sell your soul to the devil to have a so-called life in Babeville?"

Okay, she had a point there.

"For that matter, would you rather live free or die?"

What was she talking about? She'd made her point. I got it, already.

But wait a minute—I could well be dead now. If it hadn't been for that earlier traffic jam, I would actually have been traveling a whole lot faster when the wheel spokes came loose and caused the bike to seize up. Under those conditions I'd have been roadkill. Someone was not just trying to scare me; they were trying to take me out.

There was only one logical conclusion. I had to be getting close to the truth of Gladys's murder. Someone clearly was feeling threatened.

But who?

Obviously the person had messed with my bike while it was parked out of sight under that banyan tree. Could it have been one of the Mayans who had been at the party? Or had someone followed me to the beach, then seized the opportunity when the bike was obscured from view? If so, had that someone been following me for a while, just waiting for the right moment? If I was being followed, since when? Where had been the turning point in my investigation that made the killer feel the heat?

I went over the whole case step by step in my mind. I still didn't have the key. But I knew who did. Eulalia. She was obviously terrified, and there had to be a good reason.

Suddenly my Stinkin' Thinkin' dissolved and I resolved to talk to Eulalia tomorrow. There had to be a way to get her to open up, even if it meant giving her safe haven right here in my own home.

Besides, this had become personal. Nobody takes down Dirty Harriet and gets away with it.

Lana flipped her tail back and forth in approval.

"Now you're talkin', sista!" she said in my mind. "The Equivocator is out and the Equalizer is back."

CHAPTER 25

The next morning I woke up feeling like I'd been run over by a steamroller. However, I sensed that the resolution of the case was close at hand. I felt that I was now on a fateful path, and I needed to forge ahead.

I knew I'd be without my ride for a while, and I'd have to depend on my friends for logistical support. It went against my grain as a Lone Ranger, but after all, he had Tonto, didn't he? I had to admit that no woman was an island. An islet in an archipelago, maybe.

I called Lupe and gave her the lowdown on yesterday's events following my departure from the beach party. After assuring her I was basically okay but majorly pissed, I told her I'd like to talk to Eulalia again.

"You read my mind," she said. "I was up all night worrying about her."

"Okay," I said. "Can you pick me up at my boat and we'll head up to the fields?"

"I'm there," she said, and in an hour she was.

We drove out to the tomato fields. The morning fog had burned off and the day was shaping up to be unusually hot for February. Arriving at the worksite, we pulled off the blacktop onto the dirt road. We drove for a while till we spotted the workers in a far row. They were stooping and straightening, stooping and straightening. Bet *they* could use a Jacuzzi at the end of the day.

We approached. Eulalia wasn't among the group. Lupe spoke to them, presumably asking about her. The women shook their heads and looked to the ground. The men grunted, shoved past us and kept working. Then a voice came from behind us.

"Well, if it isn't the two meddling missies. I'm going to have to ask you little ladies to kindly get off this property."

We turned. It was Jake, the crew boss. His dirty Skoal baseball cap drooped over his beady eyes, his beer belly spilled over his low-slung jeans and his massive arms held a shotgun, aimed straight at us. The workers stopped their picking to stare.

"What are you looking at?" he snarled at them. "Get back to work."

He reached out with the shotgun and shoved one of the women in the back. She fell forward onto her face. Then he pointed the gun back at us.

Oh, great, did I have to pull out the Dirty Harry bag of tricks again?

"You have no business here. Now leave!"

He was within striking distance. It was time for some Krav Maga action. I shifted my weight to my right leg and turned slightly to face him sideways. Then before he could blink an eye, I raised my left leg, bent it at the knee and shot it straight out, knocking the gun from his grip. It flew in a graceful arc and landed in a pile of manure. The shit splattered up and hit the bastard straight in the kisser.

He spat and sputtered, swatting at his mug.

"Damn you!" he yelled. "I'm covered with that crap!"

"Hey, shit happens," I said, shrugging.

He made a move toward the shotgun.

I pulled my Magnum and leveled it at him.

"You step anywhere near that gun, I'll cancel your ass like a stamp," I said. Keeping my own gun aimed at him, I walked over and picked up the shotgun out of the manure. Gross. I placed it between my knees and unloaded it with my free hand. I put the ammo in my pocket and threw the shotgun as far as I could away from Jake. I wiped my hand on my pants.

Then I said to Lupe, "Eulalia may be in the shacks. Let's go."

We headed in the direction of the shacks, beyond Jake, but the bastard stood there, blocking our path.

"Get outta the way, hammerhead!" I said. He lunged for my pistol. I made a quick sidestep and he stumbled past us.

Lupe walked on and I followed, walking backward to keep him in my sights. We reached the shacks and Lupe entered one after another while I stood guard outside. At the fourth one, she yelled, "I found her!"

I followed her inside, staying by the door. Eulalia was lying on a cot in the back. She was moaning and mumbling to herself. Lupe rushed to her side. "She's burning up!" she said. "She's delirious. We've got to get her out of here."

"Let's book," I said. "You take her shoulders, I'll get her legs."

I walked to the cot, picked up Eulalia's legs and crooked them under my left arm. I kept the gun raised in my right. Lupe picked up Eulalia's upper body and we struggled to the door. We stepped out and down the steps.

Jake was waiting outside, shotgun raised. Shit, I guess he'd retrieved and reloaded it.

"You don't learn, do ya, asshole?" I said. "We'll knock your block off."

He sneered. "Who? You and the spic?"

"No, Smith & Wesson and me."

I fired a shot that grazed his right outer toe. He dropped the shotgun as his hands went to his foot.

"Shit! You tried to kill me!" he yelled, putting his foot between his hands and jumping up and down.

"Listen, shitface, if I'd tried that, your head would be splattered all over this field."

We left him to his jumping and scrambled toward Lupe's truck. As we passed the workers, they stopped picking to stare at us. The men started yelling and running toward us. I fired a couple shots in the air, then aimed the gun at them. They stopped in their tracks and went into a tizzy, arguing with each other about what to do. Yeah, a piece of ass toting a piece will rattle a posse of tough guys every time. Gotta love it.

We reached the truck and lifted Eulalia up into the cab. She couldn't sit up and kept falling over. I held her up as we climbed in on either side of her. Lupe started the truck, put the pedal to the metal, and we barreled out of there.

The dust flew and the tires squealed as we pulled out of the field onto the paved road. We shot down the straightaway. Up ahead, a longhorn decided to cross the road at that very moment, and for an instant I thought I would meet the same fate that my daddy had. But Lupe expertly swerved around the beast, although the truck teetered on two wheels for a second there.

The whole time Eulalia was slumped on my shoulder, moaning and babbling incoherently. However, by the time we screeched to a stop at the emergency entrance of West Boca Hospital with a stench of burning rubber, she had lapsed into silence and was eerily still.

I swung open the truck door and ran into the emergency room.

"We've got a sick woman out there!" I screamed.

The waiting room was full of senior citizens who looked up in bewilderment. Their eyes lit up and their backs straightened as they realized that this was probably the most exciting thing that would happen in their lives that day.

The Boca Babe wannabe at the reception desk looked up blandly and said, "Please sign in and write the nature of your emergency."

This was one time I didn't have time for this bureaucratic bullshit. However, I didn't think pulling the Magnum would be entirely appropriate in this situation. Pulling the contessa's name should do it, though. She was a major donor to the hospital with an entire pavilion—that was the new and improved term for what used to be called a wing—named after her.

"Perhaps you misunderstood me," I told the receptionist. "We have a very ill woman outside whose well-being is of great personal interest to Contessa von Phul."

"Well, that's different. Why didn't you say so in the first place?"

Before she had even finished the sentence, a couple of attendants were wheeling a gurney out the door. The seniors watched the whole thing in awe.

A moment later, the attendants wheeled the gurney back in with Eulalia on top, silent and motionless. Lupe came in behind them, and we followed them into a large room beyond the waiting area. It consisted of individual patient areas separated by curtains, and Eulalia was wheeled into one of them. The attendants left and shortly after a woman in a white lab coat, wearing tortoiseshell glasses and bright red lipstick came in.

"Hello, I'm Dr. Yemenides," she said. "What have we got here?"

Lupe and I described Eulalia's fever, lethargy and delirium. Dr. Yemenides asked us a few questions about her recent and past medical history, none of which we could answer. She then started firing a bunch of medicalese at a couple nurses who had shown up.

"Why don't you two make yourselves comfortable in the waiting room," she suggested to us. "We need a little space to work here. I'll be out as soon as I have some information for you."

We did as requested and took seats among the seniors watching the parade of ailments come in the door. West Boca Hospital E.R. didn't get the gunshots, stabbings and such that you'd get in the big city. Heart palpitations, hip dislocations and, of course, Publix war casualties were the norm around here. Through it all, the Ethels, Herbs, Idas and Harrys kept up a running commentary on the proceedings.

"Get a load of the shiner on that one!"

"Take a gander at the beaner on that noggin!"

A half hour passed this way. Lupe excused herself to go to the restroom. When she hadn't returned after twenty minutes, I thought I'd better check on her.

I found her standing in front of a sink. On the little metal ledge underneath the mirror, she had set up a votive candle, an incense burner, a tiny bowl of water and a statuette of the Virgin of Guadalupe. Jeez, a portable altar.

Lupe's eyes were closed and she was chanting in Spanish. She seemed oblivious to my presence. I quietly backed out and returned to the waiting room. Soon afterward, Lupe came back.

Another half hour passed. I was starting to get a real bad feeling about Eulalia. Finally, Dr. Yemenides came out and called for us. I could tell just by looking at her face that the news was not good.

She looked us straight in the eyes.

"I'm sorry," she said. "We did all we could, but it was too late. She didn't make it."

I let out a deep sigh. Lupe whispered, "*Madre de Dios*," and crossed herself.

"Can you tell us what happened, doctor?" she asked.

"She had a septic infection. A postoperative complication. The original surgery site became infected, then that spread through her bloodstream. By the time you got her here, her kidneys had started shutting down. The end was already near."

Lupe and I looked at each other.

"What operation?" I asked.

The doctor fixed us with a penetrating gaze.

"This patient had a hysterectomy very recently, probably no more than a week ago," she pronounced.

CHAPTER 26

So Gladys and Eulalia, both healthy, young Mayan women, had had hysterectomies. As a rule, investigators don't like coincidences. There had to be a connection. What the hell was going on?

Dr. Yemenides didn't have a clue. Obviously, there was no way of telling what had been wrong with the uterus once it was already gone.

More importantly, where had they had these surgeries? If I could find out the *where*, I might be a lot closer to finding out the *why*.

In the meantime, Lupe was having a major guilt attack for not having gotten medical attention for Eulalia sooner. I consoled her as best I could, but I was all too familiar with the guilt demon. No matter what I or anyone else said, Lupe would just beat herself up till she was senseless, then quit only out of sheer exhaustion.

So Lupe drove me back to my boat, then she went

home to pack for the guilt trip. Normally, I would have been her traveling companion, but since I myself had almost died yesterday, I really couldn't lug much more baggage.

Even so, I felt pretty torn up about Eulalia's demise. Death wasn't part of my routine as a ScamBuster, and it hit me hard. I went home, sat on the porch and grieved.

Lana floated by.

"I know you're hurtin'," she said in my mind, "but get humpin', girl! Don't let this death go unpunished."

She was right, of course. Eulalia's death had been senseless, and somebody was responsible. It was negligence or malpractice at best, sinister intent at worst. My inner vigilante wouldn't stand for it.

Before making a move, though, I had to call the contessa and give her the bad news about Eulalia.

"So where did Eulalia and Gladys get those hysterectomies?" she asked.

"There's only one place I can think of—the Isis Clinic."

"Right," the contessa said. "After all, why did Gladys give Eulalia that scrap of paper from her medical chart?"

"Yeah, I've never figured that out. And I have only Farber's word as to why and when Gladys was at the clinic. I've never actually seen her records for myself."

"Seems like your next step is obvious," the contessa said.

She was right. I had to get into the clinic and get hold of those records. But how?

I racked my brain, trying to think of a way to break in unnoticed. Then I remembered. Hadn't Farber, slick salesman that he was, urged me to come in for an exam? That was it. Though I shuddered at the prospect of a pelvic probe, I realized that was my opening, so to speak. I'd go in for an appointment, then hide somewhere inside till closing hours.

So the following morning, I found the phone number of the clinic and called. I gave the receptionist my name and asked for an appointment for a routine pelvic exam.

"You're in luck, Ms. Horowitz," she said. "We have a cancellation for tomorrow. How's three o'clock?"

"Perfect," I said.

I hung up and then I called Chuck.

"What's the scoop on my scooter, pal?" I asked.

"Bad news, babe," he replied. "That sumbitch

done some major damage. I've ordered some parts, but it's gonna be a couple days, at least."

"Okay," I sighed. "Listen, I'm gonna need a ride into town tomorrow afternoon. Think you can swing it?"

"Tomorrow afternoon would be a real tight squeeze. But I'll tell ya what. I can come get you tonight, you have dinner with me an' Ricky, spend the night, then I can drop you in town tomorrow."

There he was, trying to get me to be a social creature again. Well, he had me by the short hairs (and yeah, they were shorter than usual right now). What could I say? I was in no position to negotiate.

"Deal," I muttered.

A couple hours later, he was waiting for me at land's end on his Shovelhead. I climbed behind him and we took off. It was good to have the feel of a vibrator between my legs again, although, of course, having the speed and motion out of my hands dampened my excitement. Being a passenger on a Hog can be pretty frustrating. You get all hot to trot, and then you hover there on the verge of ecstasy, unable to make that final push over the edge.

That night we sat around shooting the bull while feasting on deep-fried catfish, potatoes and hush puppies (Chuck's contribution), tiramisu for dessert (Enrique's) and a six-pack (mine).

The next morning, I slept in late and hung around the house; then Chuck came home to give me a ride to the Isis Clinic. He dropped me off a few blocks away, so as not to draw undue attention to my arrival, which would, of course, draw undue attention to my departure—or lack of it, that is.

"Want me to pick you up?" he asked.

"No thanks, I'm gonna catch a cab to go meet my mother tonight. Her ship's coming in."

"What? Some old fart cashed in his chips and left her his take again?"

"No, no. Literally, her ship's coming in." I explained about the cruise.

"Tell you what," he said, "why don't you come by Hog Heaven when you're done here?" This was a biker bar located a couple miles away. "We can sip a couple brews, then I'll give you a ride to the port."

"That'd be great," I said.

He roared off, and I walked to the clinic. A couple other women were already waiting inside. The receptionist asked me to provide my insurance card and to fill out some forms on demographic and health information.

I sat down to complete the tedious task. I filled in my name, address, date of birth, blah, blah, blah. Under Race, I put Human. Under Sex, I put Not Lately. Under Marital Status, I put Happily Widowed. Under Type of Exercise and Frequency, I put Ass-Kicking—Daily.

I handed the forms to the receptionist, then I sat back to case the joint. The waiting room contained two doors, not counting the outside entrance. One led to the medical areas, the other to the receptionist's room, which also served as the file room. In addition, there was a small, sliding frosted-glass window in the wall that separated the receptionist's room from the waiting room. The receptionist slid the window open and shut to talk to patients, like the gatekeeper of the castle.

Well, there was no place to hide in here. I'd have to see what things looked like inside.

In a few minutes, the door to the medical area opened and a nurse called my name. I followed her inside. She had me step on a scale. I looked away while she slid the little counterbalances across the bar. I didn't need to be dealing with any weight issues right now.

Then she handed me a paper cup and asked me to provide a urine sample.

I looked down at the cup. She expected me to pee into that tiny thing? Yeah, right. My aim with my Magnum might be dead-on, but I hadn't exactly been practicing my aim with my urine stream.

The nurse continued, "Please catch the urine in midstream."

Yeah, right again. So I'm supposed to start, stop, start, stop, start, stop, all in one sitting?

Jeez, how I hate medical exams. They're just torture wrapped in humiliation, shrouded in dread. Yeah, be honest now, every time you go to the doctor's office you fully expect to be told you have some terminal illness or other, don't you?

"The ladies' room is in there." The nurse pointed to a door on my right. "When you're finished, please place the cup in the slot that's inside."

I proceeded through the door. There were five stalls and I stepped into one of them. Then I sat there and sat there and nothing happened. Damn it! I was stricken with performance anxiety.

I tried to distract myself by thinking about something else. I recited the Lord's Prayer, then the national anthem. Who knows why? These things just pop into my head.

Finally, a trickle dribbled out. Of course, it

dribbled everywhere but into the cup. Eventually I managed to get about a teaspoonful in there. Victory at last!

I stepped out of the stall, shoved the cup into the designated slot, then went to a sink and washed my hands five times. Not that I'm obsessive about hygiene or anything.

I exited the restroom and was met by the accusatory glare of the nurse. Well, *excuuuse* me for taking up an eternity of your precious time for such a minuscule result.

And to think, the worst was yet to come.

"Please step in here," the nurse said. She led me into an exam room and had me sit up on the torture table. Then she proceeded to take my blood pressure.

"Hmm, it's a little high," she said disapprovingly.

No shit, Sherlock. Ever hear of White Coat Syndrome?

Then she handed me one of those paper gowns that are made of the same stuff as tablecloths for kids' birthday parties. She told me to undress and put it on, "opening to the front."

"The doctor will be in shortly," she said, and left the room.

I struggled with unfolding the gown, trying to figure

out what was the top, the bottom, the front and the back. I had practically torn it to shreds by the time I got it on.

Then I sat there, waiting. Why is it that doctors' office staff always take you out of the waiting room, where you can sit fully clothed on a comfortable, cushioned chair, and where there's plenty of material for your reading pleasure, only to make you wait for an eternity in the examination room, buck naked, freezing, and perching your bare ass on a vinyl-covered wood slab, with nothing to stare at but some larger-than-life poster of the upper digestive tract, the lower digestive tract, or whatever, depicted in all its gory detail?

I had boned up on the skeletal system and was ready to take the medical board exam when Dr. Farber finally came in, followed by the nurse.

"Ms. Horowitz, nice to see you again." He flashed me that smooth smile. "So glad you decided to come in. An ounce of prevention is worth a pound of cure." Chuckle, chuckle. "Have you had any problems you want to tell me about?"

Yeah, plenty of problems, but none that I'd reveal to this joker.

"No," I said.

"Okay, let's get started, and we'll have you out of here in no time. Go ahead and lie back and put your legs in the stirrups."

I did so. I felt like a roast pig on a spit. Just turn me slowly and baste me in my own juices.

"Please scoot up here a little bit," the doctor said. That was gynecological code for "shove your ass in my face."

He shone a lamp up my crotch that was of sufficient wattage to light up a football field in the middle of the night.

"I'm putting the speculum in now. You'll feel a slight pressure." He inserted the shoehorn and pried me open.

"Everything looks good in there," he said cheerfully. "We'll do the Pap smear now." That was code for, "We're gonna savagely scrape some cells off your cervix."

That done, he proceeded to inform me that he was now removing the speculum.

Now, I guess they teach these people in medical school to fully inform their female patients of every single step they're taking, so as to avoid having patients go nutso on them or, God forbid, accuse them of sexual assault. Personally, I think I'd know the difference between an assault and an assessment, thank you very much. Just get in there, do your job and get the hell out. Spare me the blow-by-blow account.

"Okay, now we'll just do the manual exam and we're done," he said. Now, because I follow my own advice, I'll spare you the blow-by-blow account of that one.

At last he was done and he and the nurse left, after informing me that I was in robust reproductive health and that they would call me with the results of the Pap smear.

I stood up to get dressed. Then that slimy goop that they use started oozing down my legs. Fan-frigging-tastic! I'd be slipping and sliding in my thong underwear for the rest of the day. The sacrifices I make for my job.

I got dressed, went down the hall and through the door to the waiting room. Good—it was full now and the receptionist was busy handing out and collecting information forms. Just the distraction I needed for the next phase of my plan.

I paid my insurance deductible, then said to the receptionist, "Oh, can I go back and use your restroom before I leave?"

"Sure, go ahead," she said, turning to another patient.

I went back through the door and into the women's room. It was empty. Excellent. I went into the far stall and locked it behind me. Then I climbed up on the toilet, settling my ass on the tank and my feet on the bowl so they couldn't be seen beneath the stall.

Then I let out a long breath. Phase B of my plan was successfully launched.

The clinic wouldn't close till six, so I would be sitting on the pot for a while. What else was there to do in such a situation but…read? There had been a stack of educational literature—brochures, fact sheets and such in the waiting room, and I had stashed some of it in my back pocket for this very purpose.

I pulled the papers out and started perusing one of the brochures, entitled "Infertility Causes And Treatments." It informed me that women's fertility begins to decline seriously in their midthirties and drastically in their forties. It explained that there are several reasons for this, mainly that ovulation becomes sporadic and the quality of the eggs deteriorates. The quality of the uterine lining also declines, making it difficult for a fertilized egg to implant itself.

The brochure went on to discuss several treatment options, some of which Dr. Farber had touted to me during my previous visit. They included in vitro fertilization and a number of variations of that. There were also hormonal treatments, which were used to increase the number of eggs released by the ovaries during each menstrual cycle and to improve the quality of the uterine lining.

If these methods failed, there were a couple other possibilities, both involving third parties. If the woman's eggs could not be successfully fertilized, then egg donation could be used, where another woman's eggs would be fertilized with the prospective father's sperm, then implanted into the prospective mother's uterus. On the other hand, if the woman's eggs could be successfully fertilized but there was trouble with implantation or carrying the fetus to term, then a surrogate could be used, where the fertilized eggs could be implanted into another woman's uterus.

The brochure went on to note that infertility could also arise from problems in the prospective father, such as low sperm count or low sperm motility. In those cases, IVF was also an option, or, failing that, sperm donation.

I suppose that at this point I should have started panicking, knowing that my childbearing days were numbered and desperate measures would soon be required if there was to be any hope of producing a junior Dirty Harry or Harriet. However, I already knew that I was a freak of nature. I'd never felt the biological clock and the need to reproduce. Frankly, I think one of me is all the world can handle.

So there I sat on the john, when suddenly the door to the restroom opened.

There was a clicking of heels on the tile floor, and a voice said, "I know what you're up to, you lying sack of shit! You sit there high and mighty on your throne, but you are not getting away with this. I've flushed out your dirty little secret. You can't hide from me. This is where you get off!"

I'd been found out!

CHAPTER 27

How had this happened?

But wait. The clicking of the heels continued, right into the stall next to me. Then there was the sound of a zipper and the rustling of clothes. Then tinkling in the bowl. All the while the woman kept up a monologue along the same lines.

She was talking on a cell phone! This wasn't about me at all. News flash: I was not the center of the universe. The woman was reaming out her cheating spouse, her conniving coworker, or whomever.

I heard the sound of the toilet paper roll rolling, the toilet flushing, and the zipper zipping, the stall latch un-latching. The heels clicked over to the wall and the wall slot slid open and shut. The heels clicked to the sink, the water was turned on and off and a paper towel was pulled.

The tirade kept up throughout.

Amazing! The woman had managed to take a pee,

provide a urine sample, flush the toilet and wash her hands, all with a cell phone pressed to her ear. What coordination! What dexterity! What chutzpah!

I was almost sorry to see her go. Well, I didn't literally see her, but you know what I mean. That babe had a mouth on her to rival my own. If she'd stayed longer, I might have picked up a couple useful, Dirty Harry-like, "go-screw-yourself"-type lines. Now it was back to the silence and the reading.

Having polished off the infertility information, I was just digesting the menopause material when another sound penetrated the silence. A disembodied voice said, "Please scoot up here a little bit…I'm putting the speculum in now…"

It was Farber! What was going on? Was I having some kind of posttraumatic flashback?

Oh, the sound was coming from the other side of the wall. There was an exam room right next door, and I could hear every word in there.

I sat through several more pelvic exams and a childbirth coaching session. The nurse was recommending natural childbirth.

"What? You mean absolutely no makeup?" the patient, evidently a Boca Babe, said in horror.

A little later, I heard a male voice—not Farber's.

"I want you to know that the only reason I'm here is 'cause the wife wouldn't quit nagging me. I know one thing, this infertility problem is totally on her side. They've got a few meshuga nuts in her family, you know what I'm saying? Inbreeding, if you ask me. So what is the logical outcome of that, I ask you? So here I am, and I'm eager to prove my manhood so she'll get off my back. Now, what is it you want me to do? Whatever it is, I'm ready."

Then I heard the nurse's voice.

"Please deposit your specimen in this jar. Here are some magazines to help you. When you're done, seal the jar tightly and place it in that slot on the wall."

I heard the door of the exam room close. This was followed by the sound of rustling pages. Shortly afterward, I heard a slow rhythmic movement. It gradually increased in frequency and was accompanied by grunts and groans.

Oh, my God! If there's anything worse than hearing a couple having sex on the other side of a thin wall, it's hearing a guy having sex with himself on the other side of a thin wall. I couldn't take it!

I put my hands over my ears, but that didn't help. I had to do something.

I jumped off the pot and ran to every single stall, flushing every single toilet to drown out the noise.

The goddess Isis had mercy on me. By the time the toilets stopped flushing and I had resituated myself in my stall, the guy was apparently done. I leaned back in exhaustion. I didn't know about him, but I was ready for a nap.

I forced myself to stay awake as a few more women came and went in the restroom, and yeah, more than one made a cell call while answering nature's call.

Finally, I heard the clinic staff leaving.

"Be sure to set the security alarm," I heard the nurse say.

"Yeah, I will. Good night," the receptionist answered.

A few minutes later, I heard the front door lock. Then there was silence. The clinic had closed. It was time for the final phase of my plan.

I exited the restroom and walked down the hall toward the front of the clinic. There were two doors. One led to the file room. That one was locked. The other led to the waiting room. That one was open. I entered the waiting room, then tried the door that led from there to the file room. That was locked, too.

So both doors to the file room were locked. How

was I going to get in there? Contrary to popular belief based on the movies, lock-picking isn't generally part of a P.I.'s training. And as a scam specialist, it wasn't a skill I'd needed in the past.

I eyed the frosted-glass window that separated the waiting room from the receptionist's area/file room. I pushed it sideways and it slid open. *Yeesss!*

I could see the open-front file cabinets lining the far wall. All I had to do was crawl through the window. It was about a foot-and-a-half square. I should be able to get through there with no problem.

I dragged one of the waiting room chairs over and climbed up on it. I stuck my head through, then my shoulders. So far so good. Okay, now the tits. They were a tight squeeze, but I made it.

The rest should be okay. I happened to know that I was a perfect 36-24-36, so since the tits had made it, the ass should, too.

I grabbed the edge of the receptionist's desk to pull myself through. I was inching along when suddenly...shit! I was stuck.

I couldn't pull myself forward any farther. I tried pushing back, but I didn't budge. Damn it! I was jammed in.

Okay, so maybe I'd been in denial about the

extent of my cellulite problem. My ass was obviously not a 36 anymore. But is this how I had to find out? The gods had a cruel sense of humor, that's all I could say.

Earlier I'd felt like a roast pig, now I was a stuck pig! The first sight someone would get an eyeful of as they came in the door tomorrow morning would be my fat ass hanging there. Talk about loss of face!

I had to do something. Besides, I had a job to do here.

I desperately looked around the file room for something—anything—within grabbing distance that might help. I pulled open the drawers on the receptionist's desk. Nothing in there but paper supplies, pens, staples. Shit! I was starting to panic now.

I noticed a little cabinet on the wall to my right. I reached with all my might. My fingertips just grazed the handle on the front cover. Just a little farther... I took a deep breath and made one final lunge. Yes! I grabbed the handle.

I pulled the cover open. The cabinet was full of medical supplies. Cotton balls, alcohol swabs, Q-tips and...a tube of K-Y gel. The same greasy goop the doctor had used on me earlier.

I grabbed the tube, unscrewed the top, then squeezed it all around my hips at the edges of the window, practically dislocating my shoulder in the process.

Okay, I'd gone from roast pig to stuck pig to greased pig. I pushed and pulled some more. I felt a little movement, then a little more. Finally, I slid right through with one big *POP!*

I let out a major sigh of relief. Man! This gave a whole new meaning to the term *female lubrication*.

All right, time to get to work. I went to the filing cabinets. The files were arranged in alphabetical order with the first two letters of the patient's last name stuck onto the file tab in large colored block print.

I went right to the GU section. Guberman, Guggenheim, Guy, Guzman…no Gutierrez. I looked all through the general vicinity in case Gladys's chart had been misfiled.

It wasn't misfiled. It was missing.

I looked in the LO section for Eulalia Lopez, on the possibility that she'd been a patient there, too. Nothing on her, either.

Okay, maybe they had a whole different section for inactive—or should I say, dead—patients. I looked through all the cabinets. There was no such section. If they kept old files, it wasn't in this room.

I went out the door that led from the file room to the medical areas and walked throughout the clinic. Most of the rooms were locked, and they didn't have any sliding windows for me to get stuck in. The few rooms that were unlocked didn't contain any files.

It looked as if I was out of luck. Now what?

I glanced at the computer on the receptionist's desk. Maybe I could glean some information from the computer files. The machine was on, in sleep mode. I clicked the mouse and it woke up. I clicked on the icon for the appointment calendar. Then I entered a search command for Gutierrez.

There it was!

A whole list of dates with Gladys's name had come up on the screen. So Gladys had been in the clinic several times, not just twice as Farber had claimed. Her last visit had been about a month before her death.

Okay, Farber was definitely hiding something. What was it?

I decided to see what other appointments there were on the days that Gladys had come in. Maybe that would give me some kind of clue.

I clicked on the last date that Gladys had been in, and the day's schedule came up on the screen. I glanced through the names. None were familiar…until I got to the one just before Gladys. I couldn't believe what I was seeing.

The name on the screen was Tricia Weinstein.

So Gladys and Tricia were both patients of the clinic, with adjacent appointments on the same day. But wait…they hadn't even known each other then. Tricia hadn't hired Gladys till a couple weeks later. What did it mean?

I looked at the schedules for the other days of Gladys's appointments. Tricia wasn't scheduled on any of those days.

Then I did a search for Eulalia's name. Sure enough, she'd been a patient of the clinic. She'd only been in a couple times, though, the last one about a week before her death.

I was mystified. But this wasn't the time or place to think things through. That required one of two things—my Hog or my Hennessy. Right now, I had to get out of here.

I closed the computer application and took a quick look around the room. Everything was in place and no one would ever know I'd been there. Of course, the computer file would show the last time it was accessed, but the appointment calendar was probably the first thing the receptionist opened in the morning, so that would immediately supercede the record of my access.

I went out the door to the waiting room. I moved the chair back from under the window to its original spot.

I was just reaching for the front door when I saw it—the security alarm with its flashing red light. The alarm was set. If I opened the door, it would go off and the security company would call the cops, who'd come swooping in.

There had to be some way to get out of this place undetected. And I knew just the person who would know how—Enrique.

I took out my cell phone, scrolled to his number and called.

He was on the job at the Boca Beach Hilton. I apprised him of my predicament.

"So just tell me how to disarm this thing," I said. "Do I pull some wire or what?"

I heard a sigh so dramatic I could almost see his eyes rolling back in his head.

"Harriet, Harriet, Harriet," he said. "Did I or did I not invite you to come to the trade show with me last weekend? It's not all about partying, you know. Like, you might actually have learned something?

Girl, when it comes to security technology, you are not just in the Dark Ages, you're in the Stone Age!"

"Enrique," I cut in, "get off my greasy fat ass. I don't have time for a lecture. I need to blow this joint!"

"Okay, okay. Jeez. Touchy, touchy. All right, here's the deal. There is no way to disable the system. You don't just 'pull some wire,' as you so quaintly put it. This would have required some advance planning, some reverse engineering. Of course, some people might have asked for a little help from their friends. But some people have to do everything alone, just to prove what an independent woman they are."

I ignored that.

"So, bottom line, girlfriend, you are screwed. When you go out the door, or any other exit point, you will trip the alarm. If the company doesn't get a call within thirty seconds with a code word letting them know it's a false alarm, the cops will be on that place like white on rice."

"So what am I gonna do?" I wailed. "Wait, let me rephrase that. Will you please help get my ass out of this jam?"

"How nice of you to ask. I'd be delighted. Okay, here's the plan. You've got to wait till something big goes down somewhere else tonight so that the heat are otherwise occupied. Then you can give 'em the slip."

Well, there was an apropos term. Of course, he didn't know that.

He went on, "I've got a police band scanner in my office. I'm going to monitor it. If, and when, the shit goes down, I'll give you a call."

"Thanks, amigo," I said. "I owe you."

"You got that right," he said. "Next trade show that comes around, you're my date." He hung up before I could respond.

I sat around the waiting room. So I'd gone to all that trouble of erasing any sign of my presence from the file room, all for nothing. Farber and the cops would know there'd been a break-in anyway.

Okay, so maybe I was a little rash in my investigative methods, but, hey, I hadn't failed on a murder case yet, had I?

I sat and sat. The boredom was murder.

Finally the phone rang.

"This is it," said Enrique. "A boatload of refugees just landed on the beach. I'm watching the whole thing out my window. That is one sorry-looking mass of humanity. They're jumping off the boat, running every which way. The boys in blue are all out here—

city, county, Coast Guard, Border Patrol—here comes ABC, CBS. This is your lucky break. Go take a hike! I'll meet up with you and Chuck at Hog Heaven when I get off here."

It *was* a lucky break, although this refugee thing is a pretty common occurrence here in South Florida. Every time there's political unrest in Cuba or Haiti, which seems like every couple months, these poor people come washing up on our shores on some rickety, overcrowded craft. The media think this is entertainment, so they're always all over it.

Well, I couldn't dwell on that particular societal sickness right now. I hung up. I opened the clinic door. The red light on the alarm box started flashing wildly, accompanied by a frantic beeping.

I calmly stepped out, then leisurely strolled west, while sirens screamed and helicopters whirled above, all headed in the opposite direction. Man, was I ready for a brew!

CHAPTER 28

I reached Hog Heaven, a dingy dive clinging to the edge of town, right next to the Dew Drop Inn, a hooker motel commonly known to the locals as the "Ho Mo." About a dozen choppers were parked outside, their polished chrome reflecting the flashing gold neon beer sign that hung in the joint's only window.

I heard Springsteen's "Born in the USA" blasting from the jukebox inside as I opened the door. A few leather-clad bikers and their strung out "ol' ladies" were standing around, shooting pool. I waved my hands in front of my face to clear a path through the smoky haze.

I spotted Chuck at the bar and made my way over. I climbed up on the stool next to him.

Then my greased-up ass slid right off. I landed on the sawdust-strewn floor with a dull thud.

Of course, when you wipe out like that in public, you've got to act as if nothing had happened, as if you had planned it that way all along. So I just picked myself right up and climbed right back on again, ignoring the stares and snickers. I didn't brush the sawdust off my ass, as I realized it would provide much-needed traction.

"So, what's shakin'?" Chuck asked, magnanimously playing along with my "nothing just happened" act.

"Other than my cellulite, you mean? Listen, I need a cold one. Then I'll fill you in."

I motioned to the bartender, a woman named Marla whom I knew from my few previous visits to the place. She was basically the same bartender that inhabits every biker bar on every squalid back street of the country. Her graying hair dangled in a long braid down her back, her face was lined like a sheet of notebook paper, and her boobs sagged indifferently in her black leather halter. Her old man had just fallen off the wagon again, her eighteen-year-old son had just been busted for dealing and her sixteen-year-old daughter had just dropped out of school to have her second baby.

I asked her for a Dos Equis. I only drink Hennessy when I'm alone. She brought me the bottle—no glasses in this place. She banged it down in front of me, the whole motion signaling defeat. My heart went out to her.

"Marla," I said, "what's a woman like you doing in

a dump like this? You've got brains. You've got spunk. Why don't you ditch that loser you're with, break out of this rat hole, get a life?"

Hey, I don't take advice from anybody, but that's never stopped me from giving it.

"Honey," she drawled in her gravelly voice, "at my age I'm lucky to get paid and get laid. Anything else is gravy."

Damn! What had I just said about her? Brains. That woman had just managed to distill an entire feminist manifesto into one simple catchphrase.

All that aging boomer women everywhere wanted were those two little things—to get paid and get laid. Was that so much to ask? Instead, once you hit the fifty-mile mark, you were no longer hireworthy or sexworthy.

Maybe Hillary could use that as her platform in the next presidential election. The "Get Paid and Get Laid" campaign. Kind of like Hoover's "Chicken in Every Pot." How about "A Check and a Dick for Every Chick"?

I took a long draw on my Dos Equis.

ZZ Top came on the jukebox with "Cheap Sunglasses." I brought Chuck up to speed on the evening's events.

"So anyway," I said, winding everything up, "Enrique said he'd meet us here."

"Really?" Chuck's eyes lit up.

Hog Heaven wasn't Enrique's kind of hangout. South Beach was more his scene. However, Enrique liked Chuck and Chuck liked Hog Heaven, so Enrique occasionally popped in. It always made Chuck's day.

As if on cue, ZZ Top segued into "Sharp-Dressed Man" and Enrique walked in—Armani suit, stickpin, wingtips and all. No cheap sunglasses, either.

Okay, it's a generally accepted fact that a sharp-dressed man is usually a gay man. This observation was not lost upon the clientele of Hog Heaven. Some bozo sitting a few stools away at the bar said loudly, "Hey, anybody feel it getting hot in here? Check out the flamer that just walked in the door."

Oh, shit. I sensed trouble brewing.

The Hog Heaven regulars all knew about Chuck and Enrique, and they didn't give a rat's ass. Chuck was the one man in town who could keep their Hogs humming, and that's all that mattered to them. However, once in a while some ignorant out-of-towners would roll through, ready to rumble.

Everyone ignored the punk, hoping he'd just shut up and slink away. But it was not to be.

Enrique had just sat down, ordered a Bud, and started to tell me and Chuck what had happened to the washed-up refugees—they'd all been apprehended and sent to detention—when the jerk bellowed, "Hey, y'all gonna let a bunch of fairies in here?"

That did it. The fur started flying. Bottles broke, chairs smashed and tables collapsed. The regulars wouldn't go for the gay-bashing. For them, it was a matter of pragmatics. Of course, I had to get in the act, too. For me, it was a matter of principle. The way I looked at it, if two human beings loved, respected and sheltered each other from the slings and arrows of outrageous fortune, did the world really need less of that?

Okay, call me a romantic at heart—just don't do it to my face.

I grabbed Enrique's beer bottle, raised it over the chump's head, and said, "Hey, bud, this one's for you!" Then I smashed it on his thick shining dome.

He was dazed just long enough for me, Chuck and Enrique to make our getaway.

I paused at the door.

"Go to hell—on the Hog you rode in on!" I yelled.

Then we were outta there, just as Marla pulled a long-barreled Colt from behind the bar and fired a slug into the ceiling.

CHAPTER 29

The three of us made tracks away from Hog Heaven, Chuck and me on his Shovelhead and Enrique in his Beemer. Man, what a day! A pelvic exam, a jammed ass and a barroom brawl, all in less than twelve hours. It was a little much, even for this tough chick. And it wasn't even over yet. I still had to meet my mother at the cruise terminal and restrain myself from commentary upon her ill-advised romantic liaison.

Chuck dropped me off at the port in Fort Lauderdale just as the ship pulled in. The gangway was lowered and a throng of passengers emerged. Eventually, I saw my mother. Her shoulder-length light blond hair illuminated her already-radiant face. I had to admit, she looked happy. At her side stood a tall man who could only be her spy suitor. He was in his late sixties, with a tanned face, piercing blue eyes, silver brush cut, black slacks and Polo shirt. I had to admit, they made a pretty striking pair.

I yelled and waved. "Hi, Mom! Over here!" She saw me and rushed over to hug me.

"Harriet! What a wonderful surprise! I wasn't expecting you."

"Just wanted to welcome you back home."

"That's lovely." She put her hand on her companion's arm. "This is Leonard Goldblatt, whom I told you about on the phone. He just recently moved to Boca from Washington."

Oh. So maybe that explained his lack of a local phone listing and driver's license.

"Very nice to meet you," he said, shaking my hand. "I've heard so much about you. I want you to know that these past few days with your mother have been some of the happiest of my life. I've had some thrilling times before. But after the Cold War ended, I thought I'd never have so much fun again. Now, all that has changed." He beamed at my mother.

We picked up their luggage, then got a cab and rode to Boca. Mom sat up front, leaving me to make small talk with this stranger in the back seat. Great. Just what I wanted.

"So your mother tells me you're a private investigator," Leonard ventured.

"Uh-huh," I replied. I wasn't going to give an inch

to this conversation. Hey, I'd already extended myself enough, hadn't I?

"I'd love to hear more about your work sometime," he plowed ahead. "Maybe we could exchange some tricks of the trade. I bet spying and private eyeing aren't so different."

"Yeah, I'd like that," I mumbled.

Mom turned around in her seat to face us.

"Leonard's daughter is a construction engineer in Washington. She's about your age." She beamed right back at Leonard.

"Yes," he said to me. "I bet you and she could exchange some war stories, too. Two women both working in a man's world. And my son, he's a nurse." He chuckled. "It's not what I had in mind for my kids. I always figured my daughter would follow in her mother's footsteps—that's my late wife—being a homemaker and having babies. And of course my son would follow in mine, although they never knew what I really did for a living. Well, they did surprise me with their choices. But what are you gonna do? Your children have minds of their own. You've got to let them go their own way."

Hmm. I was liking this guy's attitude. Maybe he

could teach Mom a thing or two about relating to one's adult offspring.

We chatted some more, then dropped Leonard off at his new condo. He had some pretty nice digs on the Intracoastal. Okay, maybe he had a few bucks of his own.

Mom and I rode to her house.

"You know the big question I told you Leonard was going to pose?" she asked me.

"Yes," I said slowly. Here it came. The bad news about her betrothal.

"He asked me to accompany him on a lecture tour in the summer. It's called the Iron Curtain Tour—all the old spy capitals, Berlin, Budapest, Sofia. It will be wonderful. I'm so excited."

Oh. What, no marriage proposal?

"That's great, Mom," I said in all honesty.

Mentally, I kicked myself. Damn it, I'd been wrong about some things about him. Okay, maybe he was a little freaky with his Cold War fixation. But his past didn't seem to be as murky as I'd thought. Nor did he seem to be after Mom's money, at least not immediately. I had let my emotions get in the way so that I'd made hasty judgments and assumptions—not a good thing for a private eye. Or a human being, for that matter.

"Harriet, I truly appreciate your coming to meet us tonight," Mom said as we arrived at her house. "It has meant a lot to me. And I appreciate your concern for my welfare, too. I know you meant well. Now good night, dear."

Man, maybe Leonard's attitude was rubbing off on her already. This was not a bad thing.

I helped her take her eight pieces of luggage to her door. I gave her an awkward hug goodbye, then I had the cab take me out to my dock. I fired up the airboat and took off across the swamp. It was approaching midnight by the time I pulled up to my cabin. I downed a glass of Hennessy. Exhausted as I was, I pined for my old goose down, Egyptian cotton comforter. But the only comforter around was Lana. I wished her a good-night and hit the sack.

The next morning, Chuck called.

"Your parts come in," he said. "I'll have your bike ready this afternoon. But we got us a little snag here. The slugfest went on after we got out of Dodge last night, and it spilled outside. Five choppers got busted up in the process. So I'm swamped. I'm not gonna be able to pick you up this afternoon. But if you like, I can come get you now and you can hang around the shop till your bike is ready."

"Are you kidding?" I said. "I will kiss your pigeon-toed feet. I will prostrate myself before you. You are a god!"

"Oh, can it," he said.

"Okay, a minor deity in the pantheon," I amended, but he was already gone.

In truth, I really didn't mind the prospect of hanging at the Greasy Rider for a few hours, watching Chuck work and talking Hogs. I could always pick up a few maintenance tips.

I showered, dressed, had a cup of java, kissed Lana goodbye (okay, not really) and took off for dry ground. Chuck met me at the dock and we thundered to the shop.

There, I sat around on a cardboard box full of oil cans, watching as Chuck replaced both my wheels and several engine parts, as well as my twisted handlebars and all my busted lamps. At lunchtime, I went across the street to Connie's Coneys and brought us each back a foot-long chili dog and fries. We sat down to chew the fat.

Chuck had his radio tuned to an oldies station.

"What's with the oldies?" I asked.

"Don't knock it, darlin'," he said. "Soon enough, the tunes you grew up with will be on the oldies station. You know how it is. Our favorite music is always what we listened to in high school. Back in my day, it was all about peace 'n' love. So whenever I hear that stuff now, it takes me straight back to Haight-Ashbury. Spent the summer of '69 out there, then went back to Vidalia, only come to find out the movement hadn't never made it there. I'll tell you, there weren't no flower power in Georgia. Then I graduated, went to 'Nam, everythin' changed. Anyway, my point is, our musical tastes mark our generation."

"Yeah," I said. "My generation will forever be identified with the New Wave wonders. The Flying Lizards, the Suburban Lawns, the Boomtown Rats. Great legacy, huh?"

Chuck just grunted.

The afternoon passed as Peter, Paul and Mary puffed the magic dragon and left on a jet plane. Late in the day, Chuck finally pronounced my Hog ready to roll.

I did a few genuflections before him till he kicked me out the door.

Man, did it feel good to be back in the saddle again. I pushed the starter and the engine roared to life. *Yeesss!* I had my groove back.

I left the shop and headed into the sunset in the Glades. There was nothing but open road ahead. The sawgrass reached toward the sky on either side of me. It was a gorgeous Florida twilight. The Hog thumped along rhythmically, the vibes pulsating through my whole body. The wind buffeted past me. I was one with the bike, and the bike was one with the road.

In short, I was high on the Hog.

And that's when I got the insight that solved the case.

CHAPTER 30

I couldn't wait to get home to expound on my incisive theory of the crime to Lana. But first, just to be sure I wasn't about to make a major fool of myself, I swung back to the office to look up something on the Internet.

Yeah, it was there. My theory wasn't totally off-the-wall. A little on the edge, maybe. But completely wacko, no.

So I went home, got my Hennessy, sat in my rocking chair and laid it all out for Lana as she sprawled there in rapt awe.

"To begin," I began, "I was on the wrong track with Big Tomato. Yeah, they've enslaved the Mayans and polluted your habitat with banned pesticides, not to mention their bribes and buy offs, but they didn't have anything to do with Gladys's murder. Here's what really went down. Imagine for a moment, if you will, the Boca Babe lifestyle. You and I know it takes a village to support a Boca Babe. Indulge me while I review the cast of supporting characters. Here we go: Housekeeper. Cook. Gardener. Pool cleaner. Dog walker. Car detailer. Personal trainer. Hair colorist. Hair stylist. Massage therapist. Bikini waxer. Dermatologist. Caterer. Party planner. Manicurist. Personal shopper. Interior decorator."

Lana rolled her eyes. "Okay, okay, what's your point?" she seemed to be asking.

"Hold on," I huffed. "I'm setting the stage here."

I continued. "Now, we also know this—the Boca Babe doesn't give a second thought to this whole class of personal servants whose only function is to meet her every need and desire. She simply deserves it, just for being a Babe. It's like an egotists' entitlement program.

"So what happens when a Boca Babe wants a baby, but is having difficulties? No problemo. She just gets another servant. We already know that third-party arrangements exist. You can pay for an egg donor if your own eggs are defective. Or if your eggs are fine, but your uterus is the problem, you can get a surrogate to carry your fertilized eggs.

"Now what if you have a uterine problem, but you don't want to use a surrogate? You want the experience of pregnancy and childbirth all to yourself, because of course you deserve it. What do you do?

"The answer is obvious. Uterus donation. Just get somebody else's healthy uterus transplanted into your own body.

"Remember that 'UD' that was on Gladys's medical chart? All this time I was thinking it must originally have been IUD? Wrong. I made an assumption. How many times have I told you—Never assume! When you do, you make an ASS of U and ME.

"So, it was really UD all along—uterus donor. The Isis Clinic has been running an illegal organ transplant scheme. Taking uteruses from defenseless Mayan women and transplanting them into infertile Boca Babes. Turning one hell of a profit, too, I'm sure!"

Lana eyed me with disbelief. I could just read her mind: "Girl, you have gone off the deep end. I've never heard of any uterus transplant. You're talkin' science fiction!"

"I knew you'd say that," I replied. "That's why I looked it up on the Internet." I might have had the slightest tone of superiority in my voice.

"In point of fact, a human uterus transplant was done in Saudi Arabia a few years ago. It didn't work out because the recipient's body rejected it. That happens with all organ transplants, unless the recipient is given antirejection drugs. The problem with that is, the drugs would probably harm the unborn child. So at that point, the doctors were saying they were working on finding a way around that. Then a couple years ago, some scientists in Sweden performed a bunch of successful uterus transplants in mice resulting in healthy live births. So the point is, the potential for successful human uterus transplants has been empirically established. It's just been a matter of time till it's achieved.

"And what I think is that Farber has achieved it. He just hasn't let on to the scientific community 'cause he's raking in some major moolah. Not to mention, committing some seriously egregious ethical violations.

"And that ain't all," I continued as Lana eyeballed me. "I think the Mayan men are in on the deal. Remember the Indigenous People's Liberation Front? How I never figured out how they were funding their little gunrunning operation? Here's how. They were forcing the women to undergo hysterectomies, then using Farber's payments to buy the arms. It was a wombs-for-weapons trade!"

Lana raised her snout just above the waterline.

"All right, I just might buy that tall tale," she seemed to be saying. "But where does the murder come in?"

"I'm one step ahead of you," I crowed. Maybe the slightest hint of a smirk crept onto my face.

"Okay, Gladys was having posthysterectomy problems. Symptoms of menopause—hot flashes, night sweats, so on. She goes back to the Isis Clinic for help. But why should Farber help her at that point? He'd already gotten what he wanted from her. There's no incentive for him to provide follow-up care. It's not as if he can bill Gladys's nonexistent insurance company. And she's not exactly a private-pay client, either.

"So he tells her to get lost. Except he doesn't count on one thing—Gladys has her legal papers now. So she can go to the public health clinic without fear of Immigration right next door, unlike the other Mayan immigrants.

"So here's what I think happened. Gladys innocently remarked to Farber that she would go to the public health clinic. I don't think she realized at the time that she was putting herself in danger by telling him that. But he realized the implications immediately. If Gladys were to seek care elsewhere, her hysterectomy would be discovered, and it wouldn't be long before he was found out and his whole scheme unraveled. So Farber had to kill Gladys.

"I think the realization hit Gladys later. The poor woman must have come to understand that her life was in jeopardy. That's why she gave Eulalia the two scraps of paper—one from the Isis Clinic and the other from the Indigenous People's Liberation Front—hoping that if anything happened to her, someone would connect the dots."

I finished and Lana and I sat there in melancholy silence. I'd found the truth and it was the pits. The depth of humanity's depravity and greed was astounding.

Lana got over it first, the cold-blooded beast. She flipped her tail, sending a splash of swamp water into my face.

"So Gladys sent a message from beyond, and you deciphered it," she seemed to say. "Now get off your ass and do something about it!"

CHAPTER 31

I called the contessa. The contessa called the cops. The cops called on the Isis Clinic. It was as simple as that. With the recent death of Eulalia, which had already been reported by the hospital as suspicious, combined with the contessa's clout, an arrest warrant was issued for Farber, together with a search warrant for the premises. The authorities swooped in, with the media not far behind. At the same time, a medical team from the public health clinic was dispatched to the tomato fields to find out how many other Mayan women had had hysterectomies.

A couple hours later, I sat in the cop shop on one side of a two-way mirror, together with the contessa, watching a police detective interview Farber. He had declined his right to counsel. Apparently, his ego led him to think he could represent himself better than anyone else could. However, he soon realized that the gig was up. Confronted with the impending evidence, he started to sing like Pavarotti, angling to cut a deal.

"So you admit you were performing hysterectomies on Mayan women, then transplanting the uteruses?" the cop asked.

Again Farber's ego seemed to be getting the better of him.

"Yeah, I admit it," he said. "Hell, I'm proud of it. Do you realize the magnitude of this scientific breakthrough? This is the apex of assisted reproductive technology. I have gone where no one has gone before! I've brought unspeakable joy to countless women who would otherwise live out their lives in hopeless despair!"

Jeez, the despicable douchebag was acting as if he deserved the Albert Schweitzer Prize or something.

"And it was a pretty lucrative venture, too, right?" the cop asked.

"Sure. I paid the Indians a few hundred dollars per unit, then turned around and sold the product to consumers for a hundred thousand. Of course, the first pregnancy with the new uterus didn't always come to full term. With the antirejection drugs, more often than not there'd be a miscarriage. So usually we had to go through several cycles, just like with IVF.

Each cycle would be another fifty grand. So all in all, the net from each transplant was right around 200K. Our earnings went up every quarter." He said this in the most genial and enthusiastic of tones, as if he were cozying up to a bunch of potential investors.

I glanced at the contessa. She was sitting erect in her chair, eyes fixed straight ahead, face pale, jaw rigid. I knew if she had her way, Farber would blow out the fuses on Old Sparky, Florida's electric chair. However, I wasn't sure her circle of influence extended all the way up to Tallahassee.

Furthermore, it was starting to look as if Farber wasn't going to cop to anything but the transplant racket.

"What do you know about the Mayan arms dealing?" the cop asked him.

"The Mayan what?" Farber asked. He looked confused. Then he seemed to put two and two together.

"Whoa, hold on, buddy," he said, putting both hands up in front of him. "I don't know anything about any arms. Whatever the Indians did with the fair price I paid for their goods, that's their business. I have absolutely nothing to do with that." He looked deeply offended.

I kind of had to believe him on that one. I

couldn't see him giving a rat's ass about what happened in some Central American banana republic, as he no doubt viewed it.

The cop seemed to be hip to that likelihood as well, because he changed his line of inquiry.

"Okay, doctor," he said, "so you had a highly profitable venture going. Now supposing someone, like Gladys Gutierrez, was about to take some action that would imperil your income stream. Well, as a prudent businessperson, you would understandably take countermeasures to head that off, isn't that right?"

Farber hauled out that smirk of his.

"You are not going to pin that one on me," he said. "I am a medical man, not a murderous maniac."

Then he looked straight at the mirror. I knew he couldn't see me on the other side, but his eyes bore right into mine. I'll confess that a chill ran down my spine.

He said, very slowly and deliberately, "Read my lips: I did not have homicidal relations with that woman!"

Damn! He had channeled George Bush the Elder and William Jefferson Clinton, all in one compound sentence.

And just like them, he was lying through his porcelain-capped teeth. I was sure of it. Or was I?

The questioning stopped soon thereafter. The contessa and I left, and I headed for home.

It was now well past midnight. The day's clouds had cleared from the sky, and the stars shimmered brightly. It should have been symbolic of the clearing up of the case. I should have been feeling gratified.

But I wasn't. Something was still nagging at me. Damn Farber. He had managed to get under my skin. Something was still off about the whole scenario.

I rounded the final curve in the road and approached my boat dock up ahead. I shifted the Hog into neutral, coasted to a stop, then reached forward and turned off the key.

And then the full truth hit me.

CHAPTER 32

I piloted the airboat across the swamp toward my cabin. The River of Grass was alive with night sounds—frogs croaking, ducks quacking, storks flapping. Here and there a gator floated by. None of them provided any comfort for me, though.

I reached the cabin, brought the boat up to the side of the porch and cut the engine. I took off my earmuffs and pulled out my earplugs, then stepped onto the porch to tie up the boat.

Lana's glistening eyeballs appeared above the waterline, staring me down.

"So what gives?" she seemed to be asking.

"Hold on," I said. "Let me get my drink, then I'll tell you all about it."

I went in, got my Hennessy, then sat down on the porch and filled Lana in on the evening's events.

"So Farber didn't kill Gladys?" she asked when I finished.

"No," I replied. "It was Tricia Weinstein."

Lana flipped her tail. "Say what?" was her question.

"Okay." I said. "Here's how it came to me. It was really a bunch of inconsistencies. First the music."

"Music?" Lana repeated.

"Yeah. The couple times I visited Tricia at her house, she was listening to the Eagles and ABBA—seventies stuff. She was really getting into it both times. Now, Chuck told me that our favorite music is always the stuff we listened to in high school. So then it struck me. If seventies music was Tricia's favorite, she must have been in high school then. So she must be in her forties now. I gotta tell ya, she's lookin' good. I took her for her early to midthirties."

Lana rolled her eyes. "Well, duh," she was saying. "This is Boca. You should have known nobody's as young as they look."

I ignored her and went on.

"So maybe she could fool people with her face, but she couldn't fool her reproductive system. Her time was up. She was infertile."

Lana seemed to think that over.

"Now, inconsistency number two," I continued. "Tricia is the Queen of Organization, the Mistress of

Planning. But she told me her pregnancy had been a 'wonderful surprise.' I should have known. It doesn't fit. Her pregnancy must have been planned way in advance, like everything else in her life. No way would she just leave it up to chance. So I realized that when she told me that, it was because she had something to hide. And that something was her uterus transplant.

"Here's what happened. Tricia was on the waiting list for a transplant at the Isis Clinic. One day, she went in for a pre-op appointment. After her appointment, she stopped in the restroom on her way out. Gladys was in the exam room next door. The walls are thin in there. She overheard Gladys telling Farber that she was going to go to the public health clinic to get treatment for her menopausal symptoms.

"Well, that posed a direct threat to Tricia, because the whole scheme would come unraveled, and then she wouldn't get her new uterus and get the baby she desperately wanted. She couldn't let that happen."

"Wait a minute," Lana said. "Tricia didn't know Gladys at the time. How did she find out who she was?"

I glared at her bulging eyes.

"I don't know that," I admitted.

"And why didn't she just pay Gladys off to keep quiet about her hysterectomy instead of killing her?"

"Who knows?" I snapped. Lana was getting on my nerves with her questions. "Maybe she figured payoffs are a bother. People always get greedy and want more and more. Once you start down that road, you're trapped. You become a blackmail victim."

Lana didn't respond to that, so I continued.

"Okay, inconsistency number three. The first time I was at Tricia's house, her husband came by asking about his missing red tie. But she didn't do what most people would in that situation. She didn't try to help him remember where it might be. Like, she didn't ask him when was the last time he had it on, or what he was doing when he took it off, or if he had looked in certain places. She just said she didn't know where it was, and suggested he wear a different one.

"Now here's one thing I don't get," I said before Lana could get it in herself, "with all her planning and organization, why did Tricia use her husband's tie to commit the murder? It just seems too spontaneous, especially since she knew he'd been photographed in the tie the night before. She must have had a better plan, but something went wrong.

"Anyway, she strangled Gladys with the tie, and

then everything was back on track. She went ahead and got her uterus transplant. That's why she has a 'caesarean' scar. It's not from a caesarean delivery, it's from the uterus replacement."

Lana's unblinking eyes bore into me.

"That's all well and good," she was saying. "But who's gonna buy it? A prosecutor will laugh in your face. There's no evidence, not even circumstantial."

"I know, I know," I said. "How the hell am I going to get justice for Gladys?"

With a sigh I stood up, then bent over to pick up my empty glass. Suddenly, something big and hard hit my ass with a *thwack* and I went down. What the hell?

I pushed up off the ground with my arms and turned around just in time to see Mark Cohen standing over me, holding a canoe paddle aloft, ready to bring it down on my head. Tricia Weinstein stood beside him, her hair jutting out wildly, her dark eyes gleaming with lunacy. Out of the corner of my eye I saw a canoe docked on the far side of the porch. Guess I didn't have to worry about going after the killer anymore, since she'd come to me. And brought her husband for reinforcement.

I did a quick body roll to the right and the paddle came crashing down an inch away from me, breaking through the wooden slats of the porch.

Mark struggled to dislodge it.

"Get her, honey, get her!" Tricia screamed.

Mark pulled the paddle out and raised it overhead to strike at me again. It looked like we were in for the mother of all climax battles here. It was time once more for some Krav Maga action. I caught Mark's wrist on the downswing, then pulled him forward, using his own momentum against him and bringing him down next to me.

We rolled around, each trying to get on top. The whole time Tricia kept up the screaming.

"After everything I've gone through to have this baby, do you think I'm going to let you stop me? Do you have any idea what it's like to see all your friends having babies while you can't? And the humiliation of fertility treatments?"

Mark was on top of me now. He gripped his fingers around my throat. I struggled to breathe. Tricia continued her harangue.

"Do you know what it's like to have an organ transplant? And then to be pregnant at my age? I'm in so much pain and so tired I can hardly move. But it's all going to be worth it. And you are not getting in my way!"

"It's okay, baby," Mark gasped to her as he continued to strangle me. "I'm taking care of it."

I slid my arms between both of his and pushed outward with all my strength. His arms flew to his sides. I shoved the palm of my hand right into the space between his nose and upper lip. His head snapped back, and his body followed.

I reached for my gun in my boot, but he was already on me again. Tricia stepped closer, trying to get at me, too, but her huge belly made her movements ungainly. Mark and I rolled again—right into Tricia's legs. Then—*SPLAT!* She went over the edge of the porch and straight into the swamp.

I crawled over to the edge. Tricia was thrashing like crazy in the murky water. But wait. There was way too much thrashing going on here to be caused by two arms and two legs. Then I saw it: A long ridged tail and a protruding snout. Lana! She was about to attack Tricia!

"Oh my God!" Mark yelled, freezing in place.

My Inner Vigilante wanted to let justice take its course. But then my conscience kicked in. There was an innocent life at stake here—and I don't mean Tricia's.

"Help me get her out, you moron!" I yelled at Mark.

Just as Lana snapped at Tricia's foot, Mark and I reached into the swamp, grabbed hold of each of Tricia's arms, and hauled her out.

As Mark tended to Tricia, I pulled out my gun and aimed it at them. Then I got out my cell phone with my free hand and dialed 911. I asked to be switched to the cop from earlier that evening. I figured they'd still be on the job, doing the paperwork on Farber. I was right. When he got on the phone, I quickly gave him the story, gave him my location in GPS coordinates, and asked him to send reinforcements. They arrived about an hour later in a patrol airboat.

Ultimately, Tricia confessed to Gladys's murder. In the process, she filled in the missing pieces of the story.

After overhearing Gladys's and Farber's discussion at the Isis Clinic, Tricia had bribed the receptionist, a Boca Babe wannabe, into revealing Gladys's identity in exchange for Tricia's Prada bag. Then, knowing that the uterus donors were Mayan women, and knowing, as everyone in Boca did, that the Rescue Mission served the Mayans, Tricia hired

Gladys through the Mission's employment service so that she could kill her in her own home. The morning of the murder, Tricia intended to strangle Gladys in the kitchen with the dog leash that hung by her front door. But the dog walker came early that day, taking the leash before Tricia could use it. So Tricia grabbed the nearest available replacement, Mark's tie. It was lying on the kitchen counter, where he'd left it the night before, slob that he was. After strangling Gladys, Tricia tossed the tie into a canal and dumped Gladys's body in the tomato field.

After I got on Tricia's trail, she tried to kill me by running me off the road on my Hog. Then, after I questioned Mark about his red tie, he figured out that Tricia had killed Gladys. So then he came after me, sabotaging my bike. And finally, when they saw the news of Farber's arrest, they joined forces to get me together.

A few days after their arrest, Tricia gave birth to a healthy baby boy. She is now serving a life sentence, and the baby is being raised by Mark, who was indicted for my attempted murder but pled guilty to a lesser charge and is serving house arrest.

Twenty-eight Mayan women from the tomato

fields were found to have had hysterectomies, and all are being provided aftercare by the public health clinic. The Isis Clinic was shut down, and Farber and his staff are awaiting trial on the illegal organ transplant charges. Meanwhile, he's out on bail and basking in the limelight of his notoriety. Stories on him appeared on all the major news channels, and a TV movie-of-the-week is in the works.

The Feds vowed to zealously prosecute the Indigenous People's Liberation Front for arms dealing, to deport all the Mayan men involved, and crack down on future illegal immigrant trafficking. Shortly after these pronouncements, Big Tomato made some hefty campaign contributions to numerous political candidates of both parties, and the subject never came up again.

Eulalia Lopez was buried next to Gladys Gutierrez in the county cemetery. The contessa paid me generously for my work, so I used part of the payment to buy a headstone for Gladys's and Eulalia's graves.

On a cool, foggy morning in March, the contessa, Lupe, Chuck, Enrique and I rode out to the graveyard. Lupe and I were on my Hog. Chuck had hooked up a sidecar to his. He and Enrique rode on the bike, and the contessa, with Coco in her lap, sat regally in the sidecar, decked out for the occasion in a leather helmet, goggles and a long scarf that flowed in the breeze behind her as our procession made its way through Boca.

We arrived at our destination. The five of us gathered around and watched in silence as the engraved headstone was installed.

Gladys Gutierrez   Eulalia Lopez
198?—2005   198?—2006
Good night, sweet princesses.
May flights of angels sing you to your rest.

On the personal front, this case taught me something about myself. I now understand what the contessa knew all along: Gladys and I did have some common ground. In fact, in the final analysis, Boca Babes weren't so different from the Mayan women: they were all slaves to something, commodities to be bought and sold. Whether it was tomatoes or Tiffany's, these women were owned by corporations. And whether the basic trade involved wombs for weapons or blow jobs for bling-bling, it was the men who controlled it.

So here's what I learned: none of us are free until

all of us are free. Working on my own recovery meant working for the recovery of others. So I'd keep fighting for Truth and Justice for the Mayans, and for oppressed women everywhere—my own survival depended on it.

And on a lighter note, spring has brought love, lust and dangerous liaisons into the air. Leonard Goldblatt is displacing his Cold War obsession by dropping love bombs on Mom. Lior is still popping up, so to speak, in my dreams, so I've decided to take the plunge. We're meeting next week at the shooting range. Just don't call it a date. And Chuck and Enrique decided to tie the knot and have asked me to serve as their best woman. The ceremony is set for April, shortly after Daytona Bike Week. You won't find me at the rally, but if you see a lone lady knight on a shining Hog cruising down the highway, it just might be this Boca-turned-Biker Babe.

There comes a time in every woman's life when she needs more.

Sometimes finding what you want means leaving everything you love. Big-hearted, warm and funny, Flying Lessons is a story of love and courage as Beth Holt Martin sets out to change her life and her marriage, for better or for worse.

Flying Lessons

by
Peggy Webb

REQUEST YOUR FREE BOOKS!

2 FREE NOVELS TO INTRODUCE YOU TO OUR BRAND-NEW LINE!

 N^ext ™

There's the life you planned. And there's what comes next.

There are things inside us
we don't know how to express,
but that doesn't mean
they're not there.

**A poignant story about a woman
coming to terms with her relationship
with her father and learning to open up
to the other men in her life.**

The Birdman's Daughter

by Cindi Myers

HN38

Available April 2006
TheNextNovel.com

HARLEQUIN
Next

With these women, being single never means being alone

Lauren, a divorced empty nester, has tricked her editor into thinking she is a twentysomething girl living the single life. As research for her successful column, she hits the bars, bistros, concerts and lingerie shops with her close friends. When her job requires her to make a live television appearance, can she keep her true identity a secret?

The Single Life
by Liz Wood

You're never too old to sneak out at night

BJ thinks her younger sister, Iris, needs a love interest. So she does what any mature woman would do and organizes an Over-Fifty Singles Night. When her matchmaking backfires it turns out to be the best thing either of them could have hoped for.

Over 50's Singles Night

by Ellyn Bache

HN37
Available April 2006
TheNextNovel.com

Life is full of hope.

Facing a family crisis, Melinda and
her husband are forced to look
at their lives and end up learning
what is really important.

Falling Out
of Bed

by
Mary Schramski

HARLEQUIN®

Ne xt™

HN41

Available May 2006
TheNextNovel.com

It's a dating jungle out there!

Four thirtysomething women with a fear of dating form a network of support to empower each other as they face the trials and travails of modern matchmaking in Los Angeles.

The I Hate To Date Club

by
Elda Minger

Available May 2006
TheNextNovel.com

HN43